You Can Make a Difference, Maddie Morrison

Dale Baumwoll

Neal Morgan Publishing
New Jersey

Published by
Neal Morgan Publishing
Randolph, New Jersey

For information on this book and other books available, please
email dale@dalebaumwoll.com or visit our website
www.dalebaumwoll.com.

Printed by Signature Book Printing, www.sbpbooks.com

ISBN 978-0-9786117-1-2

Printed in the United States of America
July 2008

For Gary and Erica,
my proudest and best accomplishments!

Acknowledgements:

My deepest thanks go out to so many people for their help and support on my journey with Maddie Morrison. To the boys and girls who enthusiastically awaited my next book.

To my most respected editor and dear friend, Tess, who gave me her time and expertise and made my words better.

To my talented graphic designer, Robin, who offers her keen eye and constant support.

And most of all, to my husband, Bobby, who motivates me to be the best I can be through his love and his example. He has really made the difference!

CHAPTER 1

Maddie rubbed the sleep from her eyes, yawned, and smiled to herself. Saturday! She loved Saturdays because there was nothing to do.

"Maddie, get up! It's 10:00 and we have a lot planned for today," Mrs. Morrison's excited voice broke into Maddie's thoughts. "Dad and I are taking you to the State Park, remember? I packed a picnic and we can shop at some antique stores on the way home." Mrs. Morrison loved to plan everything so it all worked out and she could look forward to the entire day.

"Mom, I'm so cozy in my bed. Please let me just do nothing today," Maddie mumbled in a lazy voice still filled with morning. She could smell the buttery, cinnamon toast she loved so much warming in the oven and it was getting harder to stay in bed.

"Oh stop it," Mrs. Morrison quipped. "You can sleep anytime," she said, knowing Maddie was not a morning person. "I made waffles and your favorite, cinnamon toast."

It wasn't that Maddie didn't like spending time with her family. She loved her mom and dad. Since her mom had started the baking business and the s'mores were so popular, she was always happy and there was a kind of sweet atmosphere in her house all the time. But

1

Maddie loved to do nothing. It was her favorite thing to do. Her mother was beginning to worry about this "nothing" time.

"You have to keep yourself busy," Mrs. Morrison professed to Maddie. When you have a day of planned events you actually will get more accomplished!" That was her motto. Do more and get more done. Maddie didn't get it at all. What Maddie wanted to do more of was sleep, especially this particular Saturday morning.

Even though Maddie was just 12 years old, there were so many important things on her mind. Her day was filled with decisions that needed to be made. What would she wear? Where would she go with her friends this weekend? Who would be her next boyfriend? Who would sit at her table at lunch? And oh yeah, when would she have time to study for that test or write that paper? These were the difficult questions she and her friends had to worry about in a single day, especially the school work, which has been of some concern lately for Maddie.

While lying in bed, she recalled a recent conversation at the lunch table. "Ughh, this stuff is getting hard. I actually have to study for a test in order to get a good grade," Maddie had complained to her friends. "What's up with that? I had so much more free time in fifth grade. I don't even remember having to do much homework, not to mention study for a test." Her friends nodded in agreement, but Audrey was the only one who answered back.

"I knew this was coming. My brother started getting C's when he started middle school, and he warned me that I'd better buckle down or it would happen to me," Audrey said with a confidence she usually didn't have in other areas.

"So what did you do?" spouted three girls all at once.

"I organized myself with a study place at home and I did my homework every night. I planned a little time every night for upcoming tests so I wouldn't have to cram it into one night..." Audrey was cut off by Maddie's quick response.

"Oh, that sounds like my mother, Audrey! I should probably be listening to you, but let's talk about the party at Matt's house instead." Talking about boys and parties was much more interesting to Maddie than school. Maddie was frustrated with Audrey's talk of study tips, mostly because she was not able to incorporate them into her own life. Lately, Maddie's grades had been going down. She had been an excellent student in every subject, and now in middle school, it had become harder to get an A. All this trouble started in sixth grade when Maddie got so much homework that scheduling it around her social life became impossible to handle. She wasn't ready to cut down on TV or computer time. Her mom had given her the same advice she just got from Audrey. Maddie didn't embrace the new study tips and continued to drop from As to Bs and even one C in social studies.

Maddie's thoughts were interrupted when her mom gently plopped on the bed to wake her up. She stroked Maddie's hair, kissed her cheek, and whispered in her ear, "C'mon, my girl, we're going to have a great day. April is one of our favorite months. We can just grab a sweatshirt, breathe in the fresh air, and sing songs in the car."

"Just a few more minutes, and then I'll get up. Can I invite Audrey to come too?" Maddie was starting to look forward to the day, but having Audrey there always made it more fun somehow.

"Sure, she knows all our favorite songs. Tell her to bring a jacket though, it's still cool out."

Maddie and Audrey had been friends since Audrey had moved to Spring Valley in first grade. They lived in the same part of town and spent a lot of time together. Their differences seemed to connect them. Audrey was very organized, liked to read, loved movies, and loved to plan things, just as Maddie's mom did. Maddie was a bit disorganized, loved to shop, liked to read magazines, and liked a lot of free time to hang out with friends. They balanced each other. Audrey helped Maddie realize the importance of school work, and Maddie helped Audrey realize the importance of fun. Maddie also kept Audrey entertained from time to time with outrageous stories of adventures that she told just for fun. Audrey wasn't always sure if the stories were imagined or real. Either way, it was fun to be friends with Maddie Morrison. A few months back when Maddie was working on her acceptance into the popular girls' crowd, Audrey felt left out and didn't understand her quest. Maddie soon realized that popular girls were not necessarily good friends. Audrey was a good friend who stuck by Maddie, no matter what.

"Audrey is here, Maddie, let's go," Mrs. Morrison yelled up to the bedroom while she and

Audrey exchanged a knowing look.

"Maybe I can get her moving a little faster, Mrs. Morrison."

"Thanks, Audrey. It's the same routine isn't it? You and I wait while she tells us she'll be right down. I don't remember her ever coming right down though, do you?"

"Only when I went right up to get her," Audrey giggled as she bounded up the stairs to light a fire under Maddie. Audrey loved going places with the Morrisons. They always seemed to turn an average day into an adventure. Audrey was like a second daughter to Mr. and Mrs. Morrison. Maybe it was because Maddie was an only child, but she felt like Maddie's sister and loved being included in their family outings.

As much as she felt like a member of the family, she sure didn't look like one. Audrey had stick straight dark brown hair, brown eyes, and a cute little nose. She was very slender and had really long legs that seemed to be growing faster than the rest of her. Her friends told her she should be a model. Maddie, on the other hand, looked like her mom, and everyone said her mom was really pretty. Maddie had the same light brown curly hair, crystal blue eyes, and a smile that brightened any room. Her grandmother said she had a girlish figure and she'd be a great beauty one day. Maddie always felt silly when grandma said it, but she was secretly excited for that day to come.

Driving to the park with the Morrison's always had a special rhythm. Maddie and Audrey sang all the songs to the school musical they had just seen. Mrs. Morrison joined right in and knew almost every word. Maddie loved her mom's voice. She could sing anything in the right key. Mr. Morrison always smiled when his girls were singing. He never sang along, but always made requests.

As they pulled into the gate they started getting hungry for the picnic lunch. The homey smell of roast chicken, potato salad, and fresh pineapple slices filled the car, but the girls were looking forward to dessert more than anything. "MADDIE'S'MORES" were safely tucked into the cooler so the chocolate wouldn't melt. Earlier, Maddie had pulled out a couple and put them in the picnic basket because she liked them best when the chocolate melted and the marshmallows got really sticky. Mrs. Morrison and her friend Denise Willoughby were the creators of "MADDIE'S'MORES," and their recipes had just been sold to a major manufacturer for national distribution. Maddie was actually kind of famous. She was, after all, Maddie, the inspiration for the s'mores and the many new varieties coming out soon.

"I love this park. It's nice to know there is always a place to go where the trees and the grass welcome you to sit with them and be part of nature," Mr. Morrison had a tendency to get overly emotional about nature. He was a real outdoorsman. He did a lot of fishing whenever he could and always tried to include his family. "I know you girls aren't much for the hiking and camping, but I'm sure glad you love to picnic with me. I'll be over by the lake with my rod while you get lunch set up."

"Do you think Dad will catch some fish?" Maddie asked her mom.

"There's always a first time, honey." Mrs. Morrison and the girls laughed as they opened the picnic basket and found something they weren't expecting.

CHAPTER 2

"What is this?" Maddie blurted out with an annoying tone in her voice. "Oh no, Dad put that book in here. The one he keeps telling me to read." Mr. Morrison had been doing all he could to help Maddie with her struggles in social studies. She had been having a hard time relating to American History, and her dad was a bit of a history buff. He tried to get Maddie to understand how the events of the past are related to our present time. He was unsuccessful.

Maddie imitated her dad in a deep professorial voice, "If she can connect to the topics, maybe she can understand them and get better grades," she laughed. "Dad says that at dinner about three times each week."

"You know, Maddie, your father is right about that. When I was studying American History in sixth grade, my teacher told us that Thomas Jefferson was the one who brought french fries to America for the first time. You know how much I love french fries. It made me relate more to old Thomas Jefferson. I started to listen more." Mrs. Morrison often reached back into her own childhood to help Maddie through certain situations.

"Let me see that," Audrey said playfully grabbing the book from Maddie's hands and reading the cover out loud. "*What's His Story? Behind Our American Presidents*. This looks pretty cool. It says that it is about the things our presidents did before, during, and after they were in office." She flipped through some of the pages and settled on a picture of a teddy bear. "Look how cute! It's a teddy bear. What's it doing in here?" Audrey quickly scanned the page and answered her own question with a smile. "Wow, how cool is this? Maddie, did you know that the teddy bear was named for Theodore Roosevelt?" She read silently for a moment and then continued. "It says he was hunting and chose not to kill an exhausted bear captured by his fellow hunters because it would be unsportsmanlike. The newspapers depicted him in a cartoon with a cute baby bear and the public loved it. The stores started making little bears and named them teddy bears, using Theodore's nickname, Teddy. You can't even sleep without yours, Maddie."

"Let me see that. Hmm, that is so cute. Theodore Roosevelt kind of looks a little like **my** teddy bear, doesn't he, Mom?"

Mrs. Morrison finished spreading the blanket out and came to look over Maddie's shoulder. "He actually does look like your teddy. You know he was called Teddy or TR when he was president? And even though he was a big hunter, he was also a naturalist. He was the president who created all the national parks and wildlife preserves that Dad is always taking us to. See, Maddie? This book could have some interesting facts for you after all."

"Maybe. Let's get that food out. I'm starving," Maddie said quickly changing the subject. It was hard for her to admit that her mom and dad might actually be right about something. But she **was** looking forward to flipping through the book later, alone in her room. It would take a little more growing up for Maddie to appreciate that her parents were right most of the time.

"C'mon, Maddie, let's go tell your dad that lunch is ready. We'll see if he caught any fish."

"Ok," Maddie replied. "Hey, Dad," she called as they ran down the slope to the waterfront.

Lunch was filling and comforting. Both Maddie and Audrey gobbled their lunch down in anticipation of the s'mores that were packed for dessert. No matter how many they ate, they still looked forward to "s'more." The rest of the afternoon was relaxing and filled with laughs, warm sunshine, and cool breezes. Maddie helped her mom clean up and pack up the car while Audrey tried to build up Mr. Morrison's bruised ego after he came up empty handed at the waterfront.

Audrey tried to comfort him. "You have such great techniques with that fishing rod, Mr. Morrison."

"Thanks for the compliment, but I know I'm not the greatest fisherman. I just enjoy the quiet and the feeling of being out in nature." Mr. Morrison knew his family joked about his fishing failures and it didn't bother him at all.

"I know what you mean about nature. I seem to forget all my problems when I relax under a shady tree."

"Now Audrey, how many problems could you possibly have to worry about?" wondered Mr. Morrison.

"You'd be amazed how many things we have to

worry about as young people today," Audrey said with a maturity Mr. Morrison wasn't expecting. "Doesn't Maddie ever talk to you about all this stuff?"

"Not really, I'm sorry to say. I think I have been too busy at work. But, I'm sure she confides in her mom." Mr. Morrison usually left the social issues to Mrs. Morrison.

Mrs. Morrison was loading the last of the picnic supplies when Mr. Morrison and Audrey reached the car. "Let's get going, Phil. I want to stop at that antique mall just outside of town. It's on the way home," Mrs. Morrison suggested hopefully.

"It's only on the way if we don't take the highway and we go on the side roads, which takes longer," Mr. Morrison replied laughingly.

"Oh thanks, honey, I knew you would stop there for me." Mrs. Morrison gave him a tight hug. This was not your ordinary mall. This was a strip of about ten different shops each with what looked like the exact same things. At least that's what Mr. Morrison and the girls kept saying as they entered yet another store.

"Mom, this looks just like the last three stores we were in. Could you explain to me the difference and how one store makes money when they all have the same old stuff?" Maddie questioned.

"Wow, look at this table. It's from the early 1900's. I'm sure of it," Mrs. Morrison exclaimed rushing to look at the tag. She had some experience with antiques and had discovered some amazing pieces over the years. They were scattered throughout the house. Some were big pieces, like the armoire in the master bedroom. Some were small pieces, like the comb and brush set on the vanity in Maddie's room. "1870! Oh my goodness. Phil, come here! This end table is from the 1870's. The price is outrageous, but isn't it beautiful?" she gushed without looking away from the old table.

"It really is a great looking table. Where would you put it in the house?" Mr. Morrison was relieved his wife realized it was too much money. Mrs. Morrison didn't respond. She was now preoccupied with a display of items on the table.

"This frame must be as old as the table, but there are no tags on any of these pieces," Mrs. Morrison said, looking around the store for a salesgirl.

"Can I help you?" whispered a very old lady wearing a high-collared red blouse and a long, worn-out plaid skirt. Her gray hair was pulled into a tight bun centered in the back of her head. She seemed to come out of nowhere and everyone gave a little jump when she suddenly spoke.

"Yes, please. How much are these items on the table? And can we negotiate the price of the table?" Mrs. Morrison was hopeful.

"Well dear, the table is a very important piece. It's from the Roosevelt collection. We do believe it is from the original boyhood home of Theodore Roosevelt on East 20th Street in New York City. If I'm not mistaken, the items on the table may be from that home as well. We have had many experts in to confirm this." The old lady spoke in a very soft, clear voice. "The vase, frame, and clock are also important pieces but are harder to trace to the time period. We feel confident however, that they are also from the same location. We can negotiate a little on the three items because they haven't been 100 percent verified."

"Oh, I see, how interesting. And, what are you asking for the frame?" Mrs. Morrison was really interested in the clock, but thought the frame might be less expensive.

"We're asking $150 for the frame, $275 for the vase, and $250 for the clock. The prices may go up upon verification," the old saleslady responded in a very formal manner.

"We'll take it!" Mrs. Morrison responded a little too eagerly.

"Take what?" asked the old woman.

"I'm sorry. The clock, we'll take the clock." She looked at her husband with pleading eyes and knew he would get her the clock. He actually thought it was a smart purchase. Once verified, they would own a true relic from Theodore Roosevelt. This was very exciting for both a history buff, like Mr. Morrison, and an antique collector, like Mrs. Morrison.

"Very well. Follow me," the saleslady said with more volume then her usual whisper. She led them to the front of the store where they found the girls looking through some old record albums. The clock was unique in that it had bronze carvings of birds surrounding the face, making it a larger than average table clock.

On the way home, Mr. Morrison told them all how Theodore Roosevelt had loved nature and especially the study of birds. "This clock must've been a favorite of his as a child because of the bird carvings, and look at those big black Roman numerals on the face."

Maddie examined the clock and noticed the heavy black numbers contrasting with the clock's golden face. It was fun to imagine what was happening at 2:23, the time frozen on this intriguing clock.

Mrs. Morrison gazed at the clock and smiled as a story took shape in her mind.

CHAPTER 3

"Let's try to imagine the year is 1871. It's 2:23 PM on a sunny afternoon in New York City in the Roosevelt house. Little Theodore would be about 11 or 12. Wow, Maddie, he was about your age at the time this clock was in his house."

"Actually, to be exact Susan," Mr. Morrison interrupted, "He was born in 1858 so if it was the spring like it is now, he would've been 12 years old and turning 13 the following October. And by the way, the family called him Teedie when he was a young boy."

"How do you know all this stuff, Dad?" Maddie was bored with this history lesson and just wanted to hear her mom's story.

"I find this **stuff** interesting. You know I read a lot of history-related books, and I think there are a lot of people who are interested in the past. I'm surprised **you** don't find this a little more interesting, Maddie. After all, we have just acquired a clock that one of our greatest presidents may have looked at, or touched, or loved. I think it is very cool." Mr. Morrison was somewhat disappointed by Maddie's indifference.

Mrs. Morrison continued her imagined scenario, "It's April, 1871 and Teedie, thank-you for the correction Phil, is going to arrive home from school at any moment, when..."

"I'm sorry to interrupt again, Susan, but Teddy Roosevelt was home schooled as a boy."

"As I was saying, Teedie had just finished his lesson at home," Mrs. Morrison smiled at Mr. Morrison but went on quickly before he could interrupt again. "He ran into the front room to see what time it was. The clock on the side table said 2:23, and he realized he had a few hours before dinner to search the grounds for birds. He was about to run to the back porch just as his mother called down to say she had some exciting news for the family. Startled, he ran into the table, knocking the clock to the floor."

"What was the exciting news?" Maddie inquired, not being able to hide her interest any longer.

"Well, I don't know," Mrs. Morrison replied, intrigued by the same question. "I'm just making it up as I go along. Why don't you look up that time period, Maddie, and maybe you can discover some bits of information about the Roosevelt family during the 1870's and you could continue the next part of the story."

"I don't know. I have so many other things to do when we get home," Maddie quickly retorted. She didn't want to seem too interested in what her parents were saying. "Anyway, I have to call Julie. She is supposed to come over tonight with Audrey."

"Okay, Maddie," Mrs. Morrison decided to stop the history lesson. There was a brief silence except for the background music from the radio. "Oh, Phil, would you turn up the radio? I love that old song."

Both Mr. and Mrs. Morrison sat quietly

16

absorbed in their thoughts. They had never pushed
Maddie when it came to her studies, but lately Mr.
Morrison was beginning to think he might have to
start putting a little pressure on her. Her grades were
dropping and her priorities needed to be checked. They
had wondered how they could get school to the top of
Maddie's priority list. Right now it looked like there
were too many things that came before school on her
list of priorities like friends, computers, clothes, cell
phones, and boys.

They dropped Audrey off at her house, the girls
promising to call each other later. Maddie rushed up
to her room and threw her bag on the bed. She kicked
off her shoes and was about to open her bag when Mrs.
Morrison came in and Maddie twirled around, a little
flustered.

"Mom, what is it? You scared me," Maddie
began to straighten her pillows a little too nervously.

"I didn't mean to scare you, honey. I just wanted
to remind you that Dad and I are going out with the
Gordons tonight. Do you want me to make something
for your dinner, or will you grab something yourself
later?" Mrs. Morrison hoped Maddie would fend for
herself.

"I'll make something myself, Mom. Don't
worry I have been watching you cook and I want to
experiment with some recipes," Maddie announced
with great confidence.

"Sounds great, Maddie. Be careful though.
If you need us, call my cell. I'll come in when we're
about to leave. That was a warning so I don't scare you
again!" Mrs. Morrison joked but had a feeling Maddie

might be up to something.

Maddie **was** up to something, but it was something her mother would have approved of. Before her mom came in, she was about to take out the book her dad wanted her to look at. Not wanting them to know they had actually sparked some interest about Roosevelt and that clock, she decided to keep her interest in the book a secret for now. Safely alone, she looked at the cover and smiled at the title, *What's His Story*?

His Story, wait a minute. Maddie laughed and realized the play on words. *His Story--History! That is really good.* "This might not be so bad. Mom always tells me not to judge a book by its cover. I can't help it though, this cover looks good." Maddie started leafing through the pages stopping at a few interesting pictures each leading her to more reading and more skimming. Before she knew it she had learned a few facts on six different presidents. "Hmm, pretty cool. Well, maybe I'll listen more in Mrs. Brenner's class on Monday and see if what she says makes a little more sense." Maddie tucked the book in her bag for safe keeping.

There was a knock on her door, "I am coming in your room!" Mrs. Morrison bellowed sarcastically, so as not to surprise Maddie again.

"Funny, Mom," Maddie quipped in her own sarcastic tone.

"We're leaving and we may be late. Hey, isn't the Gordon's son, Bobby, in your class this year?"

"Yeah, he is. We only have two classes together, math and social studies."

"Is he nice?"

"Yeah, I guess so." Maddie wondered why she hadn't thought much about Bobby Gordon until this moment. "He is so lucky. He never has to take gym. Funny you should mention him, Mom. I should be better friends with him, considering our parents are so close, but he pretty much stays to himself. Most of the boys I know are on the baseball team, and Bobby isn't friends with any of them. I wonder who his friends are. He seems like the type to be friends with those kinds of guys."

"Well, Maddie, thanks for all that information, which actually tells me nothing about Bobby Gordon. In fact, I might know more than you do. For example, the reason he is probably not friends with the boys on the baseball team is because he doesn't play any sports."

"Why not?" Maddie began conducting an interview.

"Something happened when he was little," Mrs. Morrison responded without much certainty.

"I really could use more information than that, Mom. Can't you remember what happened to him when he was little?" Maddie, the reporter, continued her inquiry.

"Maddie, I'm sorry I don't really know, but I'll see if the Gordons can shed some light on your investigation." Mrs. Morrison was amused. "Why the sudden interest in Bobby?"

"I don't know, Mom," Maddie puzzled, "but I'm kind of curious about him all of a sudden." Maddie's interest and her curious nature would undoubtedly lead to more inquires before she put this story to bed.

"Okay, honey, have fun tonight. So, Audrey and Julie are coming over." Mrs. Morrison confirmed. "Maybe you kids could work on some new ideas for s'mores flavors." She liked when Maddie had someone over when they went out, and the girls always had some good ideas for new s'mores flavors.

"Yeah, that could be fun. I love the new peanut butter s'mores you and Mrs. Willoughby just added to the Maddie's'mores varieties. The girls should be here soon, Mom. Have fun." Maddie was proud of her mom and loved helping her come up with new ideas for the products her company made. She went into the kitchen to check the pantry for ingredients. Caramels, sprinkles, and a jar of cherries were just the beginning of the fun night ahead for the girls.

CHAPTER 4

When Julie finally arrived, Maddie and Audrey were already melting caramels on the stove. There were sprinkles all over the counter and red cherry juice stains on Maddie's t-shirt.

"What are you guys making?" Julie asked. She gathered up some sprinkles and put them in her mouth. "It smells great and looks even better."

"It's the new flavor for my mom's s'mores. This is totally going to be the best one ever." Maddie hadn't taken her eyes from the pot of caramels. "Audrey, make one for her and let's do a taste test." Maddie handed Audrey the graham crackers. Then Audrey placed the chocolate square, a toasted marshmallow, colored sprinkles, crushed maraschino cherries, and a spoonful of melted caramel on the cracker. "Okay Julie, smash it all down with another graham cracker."

"Oh, wow this looks amazing," Julie cried as she caught some caramel on her finger. "I want the first bite."

"Go for it," Audrey and Maddie said in unison. They knew they had a winner. As Julie was savoring her bite, Maddie and Audrey took the s'mores sample and ate the rest of it. No one said anything for a few moments as they chewed and nodded their heads.

"Well?" Maddie questioned. "What do we think?"

"It is sooo good!" they cooed in unison.

"Let's make one for each of us and then we'll write down the recipe for my mom. What should we call this concoction?"

"Caramel, cherry s'mores," Audrey suggested, but then reconsidered. "No we need something bigger, more exciting. It's too good for something that simple."

"You're right, Audrey. It has to be something that really tells you how good it is," Maddie said deep in thought. "Wait a minute. It's so obvious. It's an ice cream sundae without the ice cream. A s'mores sundae surprise. That's it. I'm amazing. My mom will love this. C'mon girls, are we amazing or what?"

"We're amazing, Maddie Morrison." Audrey and Julie put their arms around Maddie and they all jumped up and down from all the excitement. Or maybe it was from all the sugar.

The recipe was waiting for Mrs. Morrison on the kitchen counter with a s'mores sundae surprise for her to taste. The kitchen had been cleaned up by a 12-year-old girl's standards. Mrs. Morrison would probably have some touching up to do. The girls were watching TV in the family room and Audrey was dozing off when Julie spotted the clock.

"Where'd you get this weird clock, Maddie?" Julie asked about to pick it up.

"Don't touch it!" Maddie screamed. "I'm sorry, Jules. It's just that it is very valuable. It's an antique. It was Theodore Roosevelt's clock. My mother just found it today at an antique store."

"Theodore Roosevelt! Wow, I can't believe it. We've been learning about him in American History class. He was a reformer," Julie said with confidence.

"What's a reformer?" Maddie asked.

"I'm not really sure. Mr. Rivers was explaining it in class on Friday. I don't remember, but I'm sure he'll go over it again on Monday. I'll listen more carefully so I can tell you all about it." Julie was an average student, too. She did well when she put her mind to it, but she really had to pay attention and study hard to get good grades.

"We'll probably start that chapter soon in Mrs. Brenner's class. She mentioned something about a project coming up. Do you have one for your history class?" Maddie questioned.

"I don't know yet, but I hope not. I hate projects. I never start them when they are assigned. My mother ends up rushing to the craft store for last minute supplies the night before it's due," Julie offered, admitting to her poor time management.

"Yeah, I'm the same way. Mrs. Brenner let's us do a lot of project work in class, though. She probably wants to make sure that no one gets stuck doing the whole thing on their own." Maddie walked over to the clock. "My dad told me that Teddy, that's Roosevelt's nickname, loved birds as a boy and he probably loved this clock because of the birds on it. Did you know that they named the teddy bear after him?" Maddie added with new-found excitement.

"No, I didn't know that. But you seem to know a lot about Theodore, I mean Teddy Roosevelt. Why the sudden interest?" Julie had never seen Maddie get excited about academic things and she didn't know where to go with this conversation.

"No interest. I was just telling you about the clock. I thought you were the one who was interested. Forget it. Let's go up to sleep." Maddie gave Audrey a gentle nudge to wake her. Finally, after two gentle nudges and one swift push that ended with Audrey falling off the couch, the three girls climbed the stairs, giggling all the way. No one could fall asleep, and the girl talk began.

"What do you think of Bobby Gordon?" Maddie blurted out.

"Bobby Gordon?" Julie wondered.

"What do **you** think about Bobby Gordon, Maddie Morrison," asked Audrey. Julie and Audrey raised their brows at each other and then refocused on Maddie.

"Nothing, my parents are out with his parents tonight. They go out with them a lot. It's weird that I never thought about Bobby until my mother mentioned him tonight." Maddie was setting up the bedding for the sleepover and the girls were choosing blankets from the hall closet.

Maddie always said hello to Bobby when they saw each other in math or social studies class. He was a nice boy as far as she knew. She even worked with him on some group projects. He was pretty smart, too. But suddenly she was thinking about him in a different way.

The girls returned laden with blankets and pillows and got cozy on the floor. "He is really cute, now that I think of it. It's funny how some boys all of sudden get cute. He's one of them," Julie confessed to the girls.

"I know what you mean," said Audrey. "There was this boy in my third grade class who was really short and always sat by himself during recess. No one noticed him much. He wasn't in my class for the next two years and then when we started middle school there he was, Joey Connors, in my homeroom. I didn't recognize him at first. The teacher called the roll. She said Joseph Connors. I turned to look at him. It was Joey. He was taller than me and he got cute, just like you said, Julie. He got cute, all of a sudden." This time Maddie and Julie looked at each other with raised eyebrows.

"Isn't it weird that we don't even notice that some boys are really cute until someone makes us notice them? Like Bobby Gordon--he's one of the suddenly cute boys," Maddie admitted.

"Yeah, he's an SCB," added Julie as they all fell onto the pillows hysterically laughing.

"Well, I think I'll start talking to him on Monday. His family is so nice and I always wondered about him. He never takes gym and he looks athletic but he doesn't play any sports. What's that all about?" Maddie wondered.

"Maybe he doesn't like sports," Julie guessed.

"Maybe he's not allowed to play sports. Maybe he is afraid of getting hit by a ball. Maybe his mom is too worried that he'll get hurt or something..." Audrey was still thinking of more reasons when Maddie cut her off.

"It could be any one of the million things you just said, Audrey, but I do know that Mr. and Mrs.

Gordon love sports. They have season baseball tickets. And Bobby's brother, Andy, plays football on the high school team. There must be some other reason. I have to investigate this immediately."

Maddie's curiosity was going to have a hard time waiting until Monday for some answers. She would begin her investigation tomorrow morning. Hopefully her mother would get some new information from the Gordons tonight. Her first interview would start with her mom.

CHAPTER 5

Mrs. Morrison opened the blinds and sighed as she surveyed the kitchen. The morning sun showed all the sticky spots on the kitchen counter and she began rewashing the pots the girls had used for last night's latest s'mores creation. Finally, she was able to start breakfast.

"Mom, what did you think of the s'mores we made?" Maddie mumbled as she came shuffling into the kitchen in her pink fluffy slippers. "They tasted better when they were fresh last night."

"Delicious, Maddie. The combination of flavors definitely tasted like a sundae. I'm going to talk to Denise about it. I think you've come up with a winner, honey." She opened the fridge for some eggs. "Do you and the girls want some French toast?"

"Yeah, sure. They love French toast . But wait, Mom, did you get any information about Bobby last night? I need to know exactly why he doesn't play sports." Maddie hovered and her mother kept bumping into her while trying to prepare breakfast.

"I see your investigation hasn't lost any momentum since last night. I did actually ask Lori about that." Mrs. Morrison walked out of the kitchen.

"Mom, where are you going? You can't just

walk out with this information hanging in the air."
Maddie followed her into the hall. "What did you find
out?"

"Wow, okay. I was just getting syrup out of the
pantry. I didn't realize the high level of importance."
Mrs. Morrison put the syrup on the table and gave
Maddie her full attention. "Lori told me that she and
Gary have been trying to get Bobby to join a sports
team for the past five years. Bobby has asthma. He
had a very bad asthma attack when he was six years
old. They knew he had asthma but no one realized
how severe it would become when he played rigorous
sports." The butter bubbled in the frying pan and Mrs.
Morrison put in the first piece of French toast. "When
he was six, his parents signed him up for the town
soccer team for the first time. At the first game he
was very active on the field and began to have trouble
breathing. He continued to play, but suddenly he was
unable to catch his breath." Mrs. Morrison turned her
attention to her cooking and dipped another slice of
bread into the egg mixture.

"Mom, what are you doing? Tell me what
happened."

"Oh, well his parents had to rush him to the
emergency room. From then on, Bobby always had
to carry an inhaler in case he had this kind of violent
attack again. The doctors said that Bobby could
participate in all activities as long as he took a few puffs
on his inhaler before playing any rigorous sports. They
recommended that he play less strenuous sports like
baseball or football, rather than soccer or hockey which
have constant running."

"So, what happened, Mom? He's not playing sports and he doesn't even take gym." Maddie felt bad for Bobby now.

"It turns out that Bobby is too scared to play. The asthma attack he had when he was six has left a mark, not a physical mark, but a mental mark on him. He's frightened that it will happen again. His parents have tried to talk to him about it, but it's no use."

"Boy, I feel terrible. I was thinking he was so lucky not to have to take gym. But it's not lucky when it's because you're too scared." Maddie's mind started spinning, wondering if she could help Bobby get rid of this fear about his asthma.

"Maddie, I know you, and I have to warn you to keep this information to yourself. Lori told me this in confidence. Bobby is very embarrassed about how he feels, so don't say anything about it to him or anyone." Mrs. Morrison knew how big Maddie's heart was. She was always the one to help out when a friend was in trouble or sick, while all the others would run off to have fun.

"Oh, okay. But what **can** I do?" Maddie questioned hoping her mother would have the answer.

"Just be his friend, support him, and accept him for who he is, Maddie. That's all you can ever do to be a good friend." This wasn't the answer Maddie was hoping for. But it was, of course, the right answer.

Maddie wasn't going to betray her mother's confidence, but she couldn't stop thinking of how to help Bobby overcome his fear. It wasn't even a full 24 hours ago that Mrs. Morrison had mentioned Bobby Gordon. He went from non-existent in Maddie's mind, to front and center. This was just another new problem for Maddie to deal with in her 12-year-old mind. She ran up to get Audrey and Julie for breakfast. It was going to be tough keeping this information a secret, but she had to.

"C'mon, you guys, let's have some breakfast. My mom is making French toast." Maddie couldn't look them in the eyes.

"What's the matter, Maddie? You seem, I don't know, somewhere else." Audrey knew Maddie better than anyone else. It was going to be tough for Maddie to keep a secret from her.

"Where else would I be? I'm here and I'm hungry. Oh yeah, my mother loved the s'mores sundae surprise. We might have created the next new top seller. C'mon, let's go eat and then maybe go to the movies this afternoon." Maddie was trying to avoid Audrey's questioning look and change the subject. It seemed to work for now. The girls ran out of the room tripping over their clothes from last night. Maddie didn't even notice that in her rush she had kicked her book bag under the bed.

CHAPTER 6

Maddie looked at the clock. "Mom, where is my book bag? I'm going to be late for school."

Mrs. Morrison called from down the hall. "Did you actually get down on the floor, move things out of the way, and really search around your room? Just standing there looking and yelling at me is not a good way to find something." She had seen Maddie search for things before. It was always the same: she would come up to help and find Maddie sitting on her bed, frustrated, and just looking around. Simply moving one or two things around usually uncovered the lost item. Maddie always seemed amazed.

"Mom, how come you always seem to find what I am looking for?"

"I look for it," Mrs. Morrison said plainly, now helping with the search. This time, however, it took a bit more perseverance. "Maddie, where did you last see it? I remember you throwing it on your bed when we came back from the park on Saturday."

"Right, I did and then, I was looking at the..." Maddie stopped before she revealed her interest in the *What's His Story* book and how she had tucked it in her book bag so she could look at it again later.

"What's that?" Mrs. Morrison saw a strap

peeking out from under Maddie's dust ruffle. Maddie grabbed it and pulled out the book bag from under her bed and didn't notice that her pencil case, a half-filled juice bottle, and the history book had spilled out and was left under the bed.

"I did not put it under there, Mom. How did it get there?" Maddie hurriedly got her coat and zipped up her book bag.

"Maddie, I may be able to find your stuff, but I don't know how it gets there to begin with. How about cleaning up your room when you get home today?"

"Sure, okay, Mom. But I've got to get to school. I need to figure out a way to help Bobby and I have to find out what a reformer is."

"**You** are a reformer, Maddie. You are always trying to change things for the better, except, of course, for the neatness of your bedroom. Helping Bobby Gordon is a perfect example. Just be careful. Remember not to let on that you know about his fear of playing sports. And please remember that you promised to clean your room when you get home. You might find the things that get lost a little easier that way."

Maddie ran down the stairs with Mrs. Morrison following close behind. She grabbed her lunch and kissed her mother, "I'm a reformer? That means Teddy and I have something in common. I'm not too sure what it all means, Mom, but I'll find out. Oh, I forgot, I'm supposed to go over Audrey's house after school. I will definitely clean my room when I get home."

"Some things will never change," Mrs. Morrison said out loud as Maddie doubled down the front stairs to catch the bus. "Maddie will always help someone with a problem and cleaning her room will always be last on her list."

At school, Maddie went right to her locker and emptied her book bag. She wanted to look at the book on presidents that her father had given her. She remembered putting it in her bag on Saturday. Where was it? "Where is my pencil case?" Maddie questioned out loud as she rummaged through her book bag one more time. "I know I put that book in here and I always keep my pencil case in here." Just then Audrey came up behind Maddie to say hello. "Audrey, I'm so glad you're here. Did you happen to take anything out of my book bag over the weekend?"

"Hi, Maddie, and no I didn't take anything out of your book bag. What's missing?" Audrey knew that Maddie didn't often misplace anything. Even in her room where everything seems out of place, Maddie knows where everything is.

"I put that book my father gave me in here on Saturday and now it's gone. I also don't have my pencil case. Can I borrow a pen and a pencil for the day?" You had to be prepared for class in middle school. Maddie would worry about the book after school. It would turn up later. She would check around her room when she got home today. There were more important issues to attend to right now.

"Sure, Maddie, here you go. Hey, there's Bobby Gordon." Audrey remembered Maddie's sudden interest as he passed by. When Audrey turned to look back at Maddie, she was already heading over to Bobby.

"Thanks, Audrey. You're the best. See you at lunch." Maddie yelled over her shoulder as she rushed towards Bobby's locker.

Bobby had straight black hair that any girl would love. It looked like he put no effort into the tousled look. And then there were those almond-shaped, piercing, green eyes looking out from his olive complexion. His feet were really big, but that seemed common in middle school boys. It looked as if he didn't notice that his hair fell on his forehead at just the right angle and that the way his shirt hung out of his pants was really cute. Only last year, the girls thought Bobby's hair was just messy. Now, all of a sudden, his hair was something to talk about at lunch!

"Bobby," Maddie called to him as he approached his locker, "Hi, our parents went out this weekend." *Oh, that was such a stupid thing to say. What would he care if our parents went out? Why can't I say something more interesting? I could've said that I liked his book bag or asked where he got it. Why am I so nervous?*

"Hey, Maddie. Yeah, I know, our parents go out a lot." Bobby said with a slight smile.

"Yeah, I know. Well, anyway, how are you? How do you feel?" Maddie immediately knew she had said the wrong thing. *What is wrong with me? I'm like an idiot all of sudden. I never had a problem talking to Bobby before. He's gonna know that I know about his asthma thing and that my mother knew and she told me and that his mother told my mother...I think I'm sweating or turning red or something!*

"What do you mean? I wasn't sick. I just

34

saw you in class on Friday. What's wrong with you, Maddie?" Bobby laughed. He liked Maddie Morrison. She was one of those girls that a guy could hang out with and not worry about how he was acting. She was fun.

"I don't know. I mean nothing, nothing is wrong with me, Bobby. So did you know we got a clock that Teddy Roosevelt owned? My mom was so excited about it. I thought maybe she had told your mom. I'm hoping to learn some stuff about him in social studies so I can figure out the story behind the clock." Maddie rambled on about the clock because she couldn't think of anything else to say.

"What story behind the clock?" Bobby was curious.

"My mother made up a story to explain why the clock stopped at 2:23. My dad actually knows a lot about Teddy Roosevelt and he made the story seem real."

"Cool. Maybe I can come over and see this clock? Aren't we starting to study him in Social Studies in our next chapter?"

"Uhh...yeah, sure, Bobby." Maddie's head was spinning. Was Bobby Gordon really coming over her house? This whole Teddy Roosevelt connection was beginning to work in Maddie's favor. "Oh...umm, yeah, I think we are starting that chapter today."

"Okay, Maddie. I'll see you in class." Bobby finished getting his books and shut his locker. Maddie turned to go back to her locker still trying to figure out what happened.

Audrey tapped her on the shoulder, "Maddie,

how did it go with Bobby? You were talking for a while. Is he as cute as we thought?"

"He is cuter than we thought, I think. I didn't really want to look at him too closely. Try to get a good look at lunch and tell me what you think. He wants to come over to see the clock," Maddie told Audrey as she collected her books for first period, checked her hair in the locker mirror, and then slammed the door shut.

"Why is he coming over to see the clock? How did you start talking about the clock? I thought you wanted to find out why he doesn't play sports." Audrey was a little confused.

"I'm not sure. I just started talking about the clock and Teddy Roosevelt and he was very interested. I'm sure I can come up with a better way to talk about the sports thing when he comes over. I'm going to tell him to come over today after school. I've got to get to the bottom of this. He seems so cool. I don't know why he is so scared to play sports." Maddie suddenly realized she had given out the information she had promised her mom she'd keep secret.

"Why would he be scared?" Audrey asked, obviously unaware.

"I don't know, Audrey. Oh no. Wait a minute. I was supposed to come over your house today. I don't know what's going on with me. I'm kind of nuts from this whole Bobby thing." Maddie hoped she covered herself. She knew it was going to be hard to keep this information from Audrey.

"It's okay, Maddie. This is more important right now. Just make sure you tell me every single thing that happens." Audrey loved being a part of Maddie's little adventures.

Maddie breathed a sigh of relief. Audrey wasn't pursuing the secret information anymore. "Of course, Audrey. Who else would I tell every single thing to?"

The girls caught up with each other at lunch every day. Today there was plenty of conversation about Bobby Gordon. Audrey filled Julie in on the morning conversation between Maddie and Bobby.

"She thinks he's cuter than we thought. And he is coming over today to look at the Teddy Roosevelt clock." Audrey finished just as Maddie showed up and took her regular seat.

"Why does he want to see the clock, Maddie," Julie wondered aloud.

"All I can say is Theodore Roosevelt is my favorite president. He has helped me get Bobby Gordon over to my house. I guess Bobby is interested in clocks, or Theodore Roosevelt, or something. I told him the story my mother was making up about it and he kept asking me questions. Bobby does like history. I bet he will like the book my father gave me, too. I hope I can find that book." Maddie just knew she would be able to help Bobby. Whether she would get him to open up by talking about history or whether she would just ask him straight out, she would help Bobby Gordon forget his fears.

Finally, it was last period social studies. Maddie and Bobby were in the same group in class so she could talk to him easily. She had to stop being so nervous and just be her old self to make him feel comfortable with her again after that disaster at the locker this morning.

"Hi, Bobby." Maddie had a good opening so far.

"Maddie, you know I have been thinking about your mom's clock story all day and I really want to see it. I could stop by after school today if that's all right with you."

"Great. I have some other cool stuff I can show you, too. I know you are pretty good in social studies. I didn't realize how much you liked it." Maddie was beginning to like history a lot more.

"I do think it's pretty cool. My mom can drop me off around 4:00." Bobby did like history, but he was definitely more interested than usual, and Maddie had a lot to do with that. He turned to write down the homework assignment.

Maddie wondered to herself, *Where is that What's His Story book? I've gotta find it so I can show Bobby. I might have to clean my room as soon as I get home in order to find it.* Just then Mrs. Brenner told them to all settle down because she has a project to tell them about. Maddie focused on the teacher.

"We will be starting our new chapter on Reformers. Reformers are the people who helped to make changes in America and fix the problems that had developed because of overcrowding and corruption. We've learned about all the problems. Now let's discover the solutions. First, we will focus on the presidents from this time period. The three presidents are Theodore Roosevelt, William Taft, and Woodrow Wilson. I will assign a president to each pair to research. Your assignment is to discover all the things your president did to help America and how he did it. How you present this information to the class is up to you. But I would like you to take the facts you discover about your president and present them in an interesting way, like a museum exhibit, a video game, a simulation, or any other ideas you come up with. That's your assignment. I will show you some examples from last year to help you visualize this project."

"This sounds cool. I hope we get Teddy Roosevelt. It feels like I know a little about him already," Maddie whispered to Bobby. She was also glad to have a project that might make it necessary for them to work together.

"Okay, now that you've seen some of the examples from last year I'm going to assign each pair a president to study." Mrs. Brenner was making random selections. When she reached Maddie and Bobby, Maddie pursed her lips and waited anxiously. "You two will research Theodore Roosevelt. The next pair will have William Taft..."

Maddie wasn't listening anymore. She and Bobby were paired off! And they were even assigned Teddy Roosevelt. She couldn't wait to get home and find that book. It seemed like Maddie and Teddy were meant to be together. Maybe Bobby and she were meant to be together, too. Only time would tell. The bell rang and Maddie looked at the clock: exactly 2:23!

CHAPTER 7

Maddie rushed in the house and straight up to her room. It was a mess and it would take some real searching to find anything in here. She always knew where everything was and somehow the fact that she couldn't find this book made the Teddy Roosevelt connection all the more intriguing to her. "Think," Maddie said out loud to her self. "I put it in my book bag when we came home from the park and I didn't touch my book bag until this morning. C'mon, where is it? The book bag was under my bed so maybe the book is under there too." She got down on the floor to look under the bed.

"Yes! Here it is. Right where I thought it would be." Standing in the middle of the room didn't work as well as getting down on the floor and actually looking. Maddie made a mental note to listen a little better when her mother told her something, like how to look for lost items.

"Maddie, what are you doing up there? You're not actually cleaning up your room, are you?" Mrs. Morrison didn't get much of a chance to say hello since Maddie dashed up to her room so quickly.

Maddie opened her door a crack and yelled down, "Yes, Mom, I'm actually cleaning my room.

Bobby Gordon is coming over around 4 to work on a project for school."

Mrs. Morrison was happy that Maddie was actually cleaning her room but was more curious and a little worried about Bobby's sudden visit and climbed the stairs for some more information. "Did you say anything to him about playing sports? Or is it just a coincidence that you are working on a project together?"

"I know I'm not supposed to let on about the sports problem, you told me a hundred times, so don't worry about that. We got a new assignment in Mrs. Brenner's class today. We have to research a president and find out how and what he did to make America better. It's the reformer thing I was talking about this morning, Mom. Teddy Roosevelt was a reformer. He changed things for the better and we have to find out how. Bobby and I have the same assignment. Isn't that great? Maybe I can get him to play sports again. Hey, I can change things for the better with Bobby." Maddie was excited about the upcoming possibilities.

"I told you that this morning, Maddie. Remember when I said you are a reformer. You can really make a difference. Just be careful and understanding when it comes to someone else's feelings." Mrs. Morrison was proud of her daughter as usual. She knew her intentions were good, but hoped she would be extra sensitive while dealing with Bobby's problem. "I see you are looking at the book that Dad gave you."

"I thought it might have some stuff for my project, Mom. Don't get too excited."

41

"I'm not excited, Maddie. I'm just glad it will be of some help to you. Maybe you will find some interest in history after all." Mrs. Morrison sighed and hoped this new reformer connection with Teddy Roosevelt might spark Maddie's interest in history.

Maddie finished cleaning her room. To most people it looked very tidy. But Mrs. Morrison knew what was behind the neat desk and made bed. Books, hair products, clothes, and cosmetics were thrown into the closet and tossed into the drawers of her vanity. Whatever it takes to get her room clean was fine with Mrs. Morrison. Reminding Maddie to clean her room or do certain things might actually be paying off. It did seem like most of the time Maddie didn't really hear her, but more often than not, Mrs. Morrison knew she was actually listening.

The doorbell rang at 4:10. Maddie had been pacing since 4:00 and ran to get the door. She showed Bobby to the family room where she had set up a place for them to work. Of course the clock was in there too, and that was the real reason Bobby had come over. He went right for it.

"This is so cool. I love the birds all around it."

"My father said that Teddy Roosevelt loved birds as a boy and probably loved the clock for that reason. It's funny how you like the birds, too." Maddie beamed, happy with herself for impressing Bobby with this historical fact.

"What else do you know about the clock, Maddie?"

"Nothing really. My mother was just making up a story about what might have been happening when the clock stopped at 2:23. She said Teddy had just finished his lessons, you know he was home schooled, and he ran into the parlor and saw that it was only 2:23, so he had some time to go bird watching outside before dinner. He was about to run out to the back porch when his mother yelled down that she had some exciting news for the family. In his eagerness to find out the news he bumped into the table that held the clock and knocked it over."

"Wow this sounds pretty cool. I wonder what really happened," Bobby questioned aloud.

"Well, I don't know. Mom was just making it up as she went along."

"I have an idea." Bobby ventured. "Why don't we look stuff up about that time period and see if there was really anything going on with the Roosevelt family in 1871."

Maddie was just as curious as Bobby to find out if there was anything to her mother's story so they started in the *What's His Story* book. "Can you believe that my father thinks I'll like history more by reading a book with facts about the presidents? Isn't that weird? History is, you know, just history."

"Maddie, history is pretty cool sometimes. I want to be a lawyer one day and my dad said you have to know a lot of history for that." Bobby made all this history stuff more interesting and Maddie found **that** very interesting.

"I guess you're right, Bobby. I did find out that my Teddy Bear was named after Teddy Roosevelt. I think this book might make some sense to me after all." Maddie was not only referring to history but to this new found connection with Bobby Gordon.

Bobby and Maddie looked through the book and then searched the internet to find facts about Roosevelt and what he did to solve the problems in America. Maddie started reading aloud from the Theodore Roosevelt section of the book, skimming along she learned that his father had founded the Museum of Natural History and did a lot of important things for New York City! She suddenly stopped in mid-sentence wondering how to bring up what she had just discovered.

"Why did you stop reading? I didn't know some of this stuff like that Teddy Roosevelt came from such a rich family. What else does it say about him as a kid?"

She decided the best way to deal with this was to continue reading aloud hoping she wouldn't reveal her knowledge of Bobby's problem. This book might have the answers to more than just her history project.

" 'As a child Theodore Roosevelt, known as Teedie to his family, suffered from severe asthma attacks. He had to be taken to the shore or the mountains to recuperate from his bouts with asthma. He didn't seem to get better; the family was at a loss. The young Roosevelt was a slight, physically weak child, but his mind was sharp. When his health was good, the study of science and nature occupied much of Teddy's time. His observations and research on animals and nature were comparable to the famous naturalists of the day. Many of the animal specimens he collected as a boy were donated to the Museum of Natural History.' "

Bobby looked at the book over Maddie's

shoulder, "Wow, The Museum of Natural History? That's pretty impressive."

"Yeah, and he was even really sick with asthma. I guess it didn't stop him from doing stuff."

Bobby was deep in thought. "I wonder if he had asthma attacks when he was president."

"Let me see if there is anything else in here about it." Maddie scanned the pages. "Okay, here's something. 'When the young Roosevelt was nearly 12 years old, he took control of his weakened condition and began physical training to strengthen his body. He continued to work at being a strong man physically and mentally throughout his life.' "

"That's it? That's all it says? What did he do to strengthen his body? Did it help his asthma?" Bobby was more than a little interested.

"That's all it says, Bobby. Why are you so interested? Do you know anything about asthma?"

"What?" Bobby was not paying attention. He reached for the book.

"Bobby, you're not listening."

"Oh, sorry, I was just looking for more stuff about his asthma."

"Why?" Maddie wanted him to admit it to her.

"Well, uhmm, I don't know. I don't really want to talk about it." Bobby was getting very distressed. He reached for something in his pocket but seemed to change his mind.

There was an uncomfortable silence. "Maddie, let me explain why I'm acting so weird. I actually have asthma, but I hate talking about it."

"Okay, so you have asthma. It's not such a big

45

deal, Bobby. You can still do anything you want. You just have to have your inhaler with you, right?"

"No, Maddie, I can't do anything I want. I mean, I guess I could. Well, I'm not sure." Bobby was getting embarrassed.

"If Teddy Roosevelt could become president with asthma, then you can do anything, too."

"But it says in the book that he had to strengthen his body. He was very sick and I want to know what he did to make himself stronger," Bobby said, anxiously rifling through the book.

"C'mon, Bobby, I'm sure we can find out what he did and then you can do the same thing. Maybe it's something easy." Maddie tried to gently pull the book away from Bobby.

"Wait a minute. I'm still looking in here. There must be more about this. It says that he was a boxer, he went on cattle drives while working on a ranch in the west, and he went on African Safaris. Don't you get it, Maddie? He must've been cured somehow to be able to do all that."

"Bobby, you can do all that, too. They probably didn't even have inhalers back then. You have medicine that helps you. You're so much luckier than him." Maddie thought the book was getting Bobby too upset. While he took a puff from his inhaler she thought of a way to get his mind off the book.

"Are you okay? Bobby, please calm down and realize this information is good. We'll find out how he did it and maybe you can be president someday, too." Maddie was trying to lighten up the mood, realizing she might have gone too far too soon. But Bobby could not be deterred. She pulled the book from him and he pulled back. She pulled harder and he pulled back harder still.

"Bobby, let's go in the kitchen and have a snack." She smiled sweetly, tightening her grip and trying to distract him.

"Yeah, okay. I'll have one of your mom's s'mores." He said without loosening his grip.

Maddie's knuckles started turning white and as she felt herself losing her grip she yanked at the book with all her might. Bobby was caught off guard and slipped off the couch. Maddie fell backward onto the floor, her head just missing the coffee table as the book came loose and flew up in the air across the room.

The book seemed to move in slow motion. Maddie and Bobby fumbled to regain their bearings. They followed the book's flight with their eyes as they stood in a room filled with silent anticipation.

"Oh no, it's going to hit the clock!" Maddie broke the frozen silence with a shrill voice that was unfamiliar to her. It was a direct hit. The Theodore Roosevelt, antique clock toppled to the edge of the pedestal table as the book skimmed across the wood floor. The clock hung on for just enough time to allow Bobby and Maddie a chance to make a clock-saving leap to stop it from falling to the floor. It was like two opposing football players headed for the same ball. They dove for the clock unaware of each other's presence. Just as they each grabbed hold of the clock, their foreheads crashed together like two bowling balls.

Their argument stopped at that very moment and so did time...

CHAPTER 8

Maddie came to first. She tried to prop herself up on one elbow, but slumped back to the floor. Then, slowly she sat up and looked around.

"What happened? Bobby, where are you? What happened?" she asked again. Hazy memories arguing with Bobby over the book began to take shape. But then the rest was foggy. "Bobby," Maddie called again and then as she looked around her instincts told her to whisper. "C'mon, Bobby, answer me. You're scaring me now," Maddie whispered and began to walk around slowly. Her fear grew both because she couldn't find Bobby and she had no idea where she was! Everything looked strange and the furnishings look old. She felt like she was in one of those stores from the antique mall her mom loved so much.

Maddie scanned the room looking for something familiar. "Ooh," she yelled forgetting to stifle herself. Maddie tripped on the leg of an ornate piano and tumbled onto a chair. It was a very scratchy landing.

"Yeesh, how could anyone sit in such an uncomfortable chair? This cushion feels like the horse I rode last summer at camp," she whined as she looked around the room. "And, where is Bobby?" Maddie slowly pulled herself out of the chair and looked for a phone, thinking she might need some help. There was a loud groan. She wasn't sure where it came from so she listened for another sound. There it was again. It came from behind the couch by the front window. She shielded her eyes from the afternoon sun streaming through the window. She hoped it was Bobby behind the couch and tiptoed over to get a better look.

Then from another room came the soft rumbling of someone coming down the stairs. Maddie still had no idea where she was or if it even was Bobby behind the couch. The rumbling sound got louder and instinct told her to duck behind the couch no matter what she found.

"Maddie, where have you been? Where are we? What happened? My head is killing me." Thank god it was Bobby. But he was still groggy. He had more questions, but Maddie clamped her hand over his mouth to keep him quiet.

"Shhh, someone is coming," she whispered and gave a look that said I don't know what is happening, either.

But Bobby was too curious to keep quiet. He struggled to break free from her grasp just as they heard someone enter the room.

"Owww," Maddie screamed. Bobby had bitten her. She quickly covered her own mouth, but it was too late. "Someone is in here," Maddie mouthed to Bobby who had forgotten all his questions and peeked his head up to look over the couch. He found himself face to face with a boy, poised on the couch cushion, who looked as shocked as he did.

"AHHHH," they yelled out, fell backwards, and jumped back up to look straight at each other again. Then, the boy slipped off the couch and fell against an end table, which among other things held a fragile-looking vase.

"Oh, no!" Maddie dove to catch the vase but again it was too late. It smashed into pieces on the floor amidst the other items from the table. Still dazed, she instinctively reached to pick up the glass and finally found something familiar in the room.

She looked at the object in her hands and slowly turned to show it to Bobby. He met her glance and then they both looked at the strange boy. "Bobby, it's Teddy's clock!"

"How do you know my name?" The boy asked with a puzzled stare.

"Oh...my...gosh. Look at the time," Maddie said to Bobby ignoring the boy's question. "It's 2:23! This is totally weird, Bobby. **What is going on**?" she said each word deliberately and then turned to confront the boy.

"Who are you? And where are we, anyway?"

"I think I should ask **you** that question. You have both entered my home without my knowledge and have broken my mother's porcelain vase and most likely caused my favorite clock to stop working." He eyed the clock in Maddie's hand.

"I don't know how we got here." Maddie remembered what had happened. "We were working on a report on Teddy Roosevelt and we started arguing over a book."

"Right," Bobby continued. "I wanted to look at the book and you wouldn't give it back to me and then somehow it flew across the room right at Teddy's clock."

Once again Maddie and Bobby looked at each other, at the clock, and at the boy. Everyone was confused.

"Well, it seems you have found your way into my home. And for some reason you know who I am. But I am at a disadvantage because I do not have the slightest idea who you are."

"But we **don't** know who you are. We don't even know **where** we are," Maddie replied with concern.

"Please tell me your names immediately and where you hail from."

"My name is Maddie Morrison and this is Bobby Gordon," she said flustered.

"We both live in New Jersey and we are in seventh grade at Spring Valley Middle School," Bobby added still a little out of breath from the confrontation with this strange, but polite boy.

"I would say it is a pleasure to meet you, but under these circumstances I think I should call for my father and mother to discuss the consequences of your barging into our home unannounced. And I wonder how you arrived here all the way from the state of New Jersey."

"Please don't call anyone yet. We really didn't mean to barge in. We aren't really sure how we got here. Couldn't you just tell us where we are and who you are?" Maddie was beginning to get very nervous, but at the same time she felt something familiar and comfortable.

"My name is Theodore Roosevelt, Jr. of course. My family calls me Teedie. You are in our home in New York City." The boy finally shed some light on the situation.

Maddie and Bobby looked at each other and their mouths dropped open. They couldn't say anything for a while. They looked at Teddy and they both said at the same time, "This is awesome!"

"This is wild. This is crazy. This can't be true. Okay, what is really happening? Are we on TV?" Bobby started looking around for hidden cameras.

"I don't completely understand these words you are saying, Robert, but it is certainly true. This is my home." Teddy replied in the formal tone that was used by the fine families of the time.

"But the clock, Bobby. It is Teddy Roosevelt's clock and it stopped at 2:23," Maddie confirmed. *My mother just bought this clock at that little antique shop on the way home from our picnic the other day.* Maddie thought trying to put the pieces together to this intriguing puzzle.

"Yes, it is my clock and unfortunately it has stopped. I hope I don't receive consequences for this mishap." Teddy was examining the clock for ways to fix it before his mother found it. "Now I must ask again. Why are you two in my home and hiding behind the settee? I don't have many acquaintances outside the family, and although I would enjoy the camaraderie, I must know something about you and your family before we pursue our friendship. I am headed outdoors to do some bird watching, if you two would like to join me, maybe you can provide a plausible explanation. I've wasted quite a bit of time already and I have to get my exercise session completed before dinner."

"Okay, I have to ask. What year is this?" Maddie had the strange sense that if this boy was really Teddy Roosevelt, then they were not in 2003 anymore.

Teddy looked at her baffled, "What an unusual question. I'm sure it is the same year in your state of New Jersey. It's 1871, of course."

CHAPTER 9

Teddy bounded out the front door of the large home at 28 East 20th Street in the center of Manhattan. It seemed the young boy was determined to stick to his schedule, no matter how unusual the interruptions might be. Maddie and Bobby followed hesitantly because they really weren't sure what else to do.

"I have always had a keen interest in nature, animals, and the like. Bird watching in the early spring is a favorite pastime of mine that I can easily do right here in New York City." Teddy was 12 years old and spent much of his free time studying nature and most recently, strengthening his frail body. "Of course, lately I haven't had as much time to devote to my nature studies. Father has instilled in me the motivation to build up my weakened body. Each time I suffered from my attacks, my family had to put a tremendous effort towards helping me regain my health. It is high time that I take on the responsibility myself."

"What kind of attacks do you have, Teddy?" Maddie knew from her reading that he must be talking about the asthma.

Teddy momentarily forgot about investigating the reasons for Maddie and Bobby's intrusion, "Call me Teedie, everyone does. Well, it's asthma, I'm afraid.

Without a cure, other than treating symptoms with trips to the seashore or the mountains, I have resigned myself to building my strength and expanding my chest through exercise. I will improve my breathing, control my body, and thus my health, and as a result my future." Teddy was a determined boy. Of course the family's wealth afforded him an in-home gymnasium that could rival any commercial facility. But money doesn't buy spirit, and Teddy Roosevelt, even at 12 years old, had more spirit than anyone Maddie or Bobby had ever met.

"Wow, man, you are funny. How can you fix your asthma by exercising? Isn't the exercising causing you to **have** breathing problems?" Bobby forgot about the strange circumstances that had him talking to Teddy Roosevelt and was more interested in Teddy's approach to fighting his asthma.

Teddy looked through his binoculars and spotted something on a tree at the far end of the property. He answered Bobby without looking away from his find. "First of all, Robert, I am not yet a man, but I look forward to being a great man like my father one day. As for the exercises, you will find they strengthen muscles, which in turn build up the capacity to withstand activity and thus my breathing is more under my control. Father was right, of course, when he told me that without the help of the body, the mind cannot go as far as it should. Since my mind is sharp, I needed to work on getting my body in peak condition. He said to me that you must make your body! And so I have taken on the challenge. Come with me, Robert, and I'll show you. It's time to start my daily program." Teddy swung his binoculars around his neck and walked with a determined stride back in the house and towards the family gymnasium.

Once again both Maddie and Bobby followed Teddy out of curiosity. Bobby was looking for answers to his asthma questions and not so much wondering what they were doing here and how they actually got there. Maddie's thoughts went in a different direction.

There must be a reason we've been sent to this time period, Maddie thought to herself. *Teddy Roosevelt is only a 12-year-old boy, like us. I need to know about him for my social studies report. He won't know any of that stuff yet. But when Bobby and I were fighting over the book, we were more interested in how he overcame his asthma. Okay, so that's why we're here, to help Bobby with the fear of his asthma attacks. That's good. I have been working on helping Bobby and now he is getting help. It makes sense now. Wait a minute, none of this makes sense. What am I doing thinking about my history report when I may never get home again. I live in 2003 and I'm about to go watch my new friend, Teddy Roosevelt, exercise in his home in THE YEAR 1871!!!*

"**STOP!**" Maddie yelled. "What are we doing here? Bobby, really, what is going on? It's 1871 and we're hanging out with Teddy Roosevelt. He's our age and he's nice and all, but he talks funny and, well...**IT'S 1871!**"

Maddie snapped Bobby out of his quest for asthma answers with the "reality" of the situation. "I know, Maddie. You're right, 1871, this is crazy. How did we get here, really? Should we leave Teddy's house and try to find a way home? Or maybe Teddy can help us. Do you think we will ever get home? This may sound crazy but I'm not even sure if I want to go home yet, Maddie. Couldn't we stay and watch him a while and then figure out this whole thing? I don't know how this is all happening, but you have to admit that it's probably the coolest thing that has ever happened to us. If it's really happening, I'm not sure I even believe we're here." Teddy turned to see where they were and Bobby said to Maddie in confidence, "We'll figure it out. For now, maybe I can get some help controlling my asthma." Maddie calmed down a little bit and decided to help Bobby get the answers he needed. Once he felt better about his asthma, they would be able to figure out what they were going to do next.

After a short stint on the horizontal bars, some weight lifting, and a bout with the punching bag, Teddy felt good and Bobby felt inspired.

"Good training, ay, Robert? Everyday I feel better. Sometimes it's just a slight improvement, but mostly I know in my mind that I alone have the ability to change the course of my existence, and I have begun to take control."

Bobby had never been so pumped up. He was almost short of breath from the excitement. Maddie gave him a pat on the back to show support and encouragement.

"Maddie, I think I can fix my asthma problem. Look at Teddy. He's smaller than me and looks skinny and weak. But the way he talks, he sounds like a hulky, body builder with strength and confidence. I'm in better shape than he is to start. I'm sure I can take control of my situation and "breath" new life into my body." Bobby's play on words was intentional. He meant what he was saying more than he had ever meant anything.

"Of course you can, Bobby. This is so cool. I wasn't sure how to help you get the confidence, but once again Teddy Roosevelt makes the connection for us." Maddie immediately realized she had revealed too much about her knowledge of Bobby's condition. She suddenly showed great interest in the horizontal bars.

"What do you mean you weren't sure how to help me? What made you think I needed help?" Bobby turned to Maddie. Just at that same moment Mrs. Roosevelt called to Teddy from the parlor and took the attention away from Maddie.

"Teedie, my boy, when you have finished your exercises please get ready for dinner which will be promptly at 6:00."

"Robert, Madeline, you must be on your way. It's time to return to your homes in New Jersey. I'm still unsure of how you came to be in my home but it has been delightful to meet you both. I must, however, prepare for dinner. Please stop by again tomorrow to fully explain your background and how you came to be here today." Teddy didn't seem to think much of this strange encounter. Maybe it's because he felt comfortable with Bobby and Maddie and didn't feel threatened by their untimely arrival.

"It's not Madeline, it's just plain Maddie. But, anyway, we can't go home, Teddy, I mean Teedie. We don't live here...now. We, uhmm, we are from...well, we are not from here." Maddie turned to Bobby for help but he shrugged his shoulders, also unsure of what to say.

"Robert, surely, as the male in this friendship, you can take the lead and make sure Madeline, pardon me, Maddie and you return home safely." Teddy was preoccupied with straightening his equipment and getting ready to leave the gymnasium. He was unaware that Maddie and Bobby were flustered and arguing quietly as to how they should proceed.

"Listen, Teedie, we don't know how we got in your house. You must've realized that we kinda just, you know, appeared. We were at Maddie's house one minute and we blacked out or something freaky happened and then we woke up in your living room," Bobby explained. "You told us it's 1871, right? Well, we live in the year 2003 in New Jersey. So it's not so much that we don't know how to get back to New Jersey; it's more like we don't know how to go forward- - back to 2003."

Teddy was spellbound while listening to Bobby's explanation, "Robert, I don't understand you. Your language is strange to me. It must be a local dialect used in New Jersey. What does it mean when you say freaky or that you live in the year 2003? Is there some alternate meaning that would make sense to my mind?"

"Probably not, because it doesn't make sense to my mind. Really, we are from the year 2003, 132 years from now. We are even studying you in our American history class." Bobby turned to Maddie to help out.

"Look, Teedie, it's true we are from 2003." Maddie tried to make sense of it all, but there was no sense to it. "This is totally cool and all, but we are a little scared because if we don't get back home, we won't be there anymore. We will never have existed if we grow up here and then die before we are even born in 1990. Well maybe we do exist but my parents aren't even born yet so how am I here?...and well, I don't know what I'm saying anymore, I don't know what to do. I do know this time travel stuff can have consequences and I don't want to change anything you've done. You, Teddy Roosevelt, are a great man!" Maddie stopped, took a breath, and finally looked at Teddy.

Teddy's head tilted, his mouth hung open, and he stepped back to catch his balance. After a moment of confused silence, Teddy began to formulate questions about things he could understand. "Again you call me a man, when in fact I am a boy about your age, I imagine," he paused. "You bring up so many questions that I find impossible to answer. This puts me in an unusual position. I can almost certainly answer any question with the right tools and information. I am, however, without the needed information." Teddy sat down to think while Maddie and Bobby slumped down next to him, all three in deep thought. Then, they each spoke at the same time.

"Do you have any books on time travel, Teedie?" Maddie thought that Teddy was so smart he could figure it all out.

"Maddie, let's retrace our steps right before we got here and see if we can come up with how it happened." Bobby was replaying the book argument over in his mind.

"Why would you be studying **me** in your American history class in the year 2003?" Teddy finally digested what Bobby had said earlier.

There was silence for a moment then Bobby began, "You are the greatest..." Maddie suddenly elbowed Bobby so hard that he fell sideways and landed backwards. Maddie had to quickly lean over and put her hand over his mouth to shut him up.

Maddie tried to finish Bobby's explanation without revealing future events and shocking Teddy even more by giving away information he shouldn't know yet. "We were studying influential families of the 1800's and your father's contributions to New York City. Helping homeless young boys with the Children's Aid Society and founding the Museum of Natural History were very important. We are going to the Museum of Natural History on our class trip next month. There are so many things there that you would love, Teedie. So anyway, yeah, that's what we were studying in school. Right, Bobby?" Maddie used facts she remembered from the book her dad gave her to keep from saying something that could change the course of history. Teddy Roosevelt should not know what is going to happen in his life. Maddie didn't want to cause any changes by revealing something that hasn't happened yet in the great life to come for this wonderful man and president. Maddie would soon realize that history **was** pretty cool and her dad might even know what he was talking about.

Bobby was regaining his composure after Maddie's assault and he looked at her with a confused and baffled expression that had appeared on his face too many times in just the past couple of hours. "What are you doing, Maddie? Why don't you tell him the real..." Bobby got another jab and a look from Maddie he had never seen before.

"Bobby, can we talk for a minute? Excuse us, Teedie, we will be right back." Maddie continued to talk to Bobby through clenched teeth as she pulled him out into the hallway of the Roosevelt's townhouse. "What are you doing? We can't tell Teddy anything he doesn't know already."

"But he's so smart, Maddie, he knows everything."

"Stop being so dense. He might be smart, but he's still only 12. I'm talking about things that haven't happened to him yet." Maddie went on to explain how time travel can affect the future. "We can't let our visit here change anything because we are talking about American history, world history even."

"Okay, I get it. But how are we going to get home, Maddie?" As anxious as Bobby was about figuring out how to get home, the confidence he gained from Teddy's fight against asthma took over his thoughts. "I want to join spring baseball before I miss too much of the season." In a very short time, Bobby's fears about his asthma had been put to rest after seeing the strength and perseverance in Teddy Roosevelt. Things seem to happen so quickly when your time is not your own. "If Teddy can exercise like he does, hunt and ride, and fight in wars, and become a great president like he will, then I can play baseball or soccer. Don't you think, Maddie?"

Maddie was smiling from ear to ear and for a

moment forgot about their timely predicament. Bobby had finally gained confidence in himself and would be better off in every way now. "I don't **think** so, Bobby, I **know** so!" *Why didn't we realize this kind of stuff in our own time? I feel like we have some kind of special ability to see things more clearly here. It must happen when you step out of your own life for a moment, or for a hundred years or so.*

"Thanks, Maddie. You know I never realized how cool you were. I can really talk to you about stuff and well, I don't know it's...well, you know." Bobby couldn't find the words to thank Maddie for caring about him. A good friend is something we all want and when you discover you have one who will be there for you and make you feel special, it's hard to tell them how you feel, especially when you're 12.

"I think I **do** know, Bobby." Maddie gave Bobby a pat on his shoulder and Bobby responded with a gentle punch to her upper arm. They exchanged a few more nudges and pokes until they just stood there laughing. Finally, they settled down and had a moment of awkward silence. The moment of silence gave them a chance to reflect on the fact that they both knew they had found a true friend.

Maddie and Bobby looked thoughtfully around the room and then looked at each other and in another moment they sighed in unison, "Okay, what happens now?"

Maddie decided, "We have to figure out how to get home."

They went back to ask Teddy for help, but he wasn't there.

CHAPTER 10

"Maybe he went to get ready for dinner. It seems like they really stick to a schedule around here." Bobby assumed as he looked around the empty gymnasium.

"But we have to figure things out, Bobby. Teddy is so smart maybe he can help us. On the other hand, he probably doesn't even believe that we are from another time period and hey, wait a minute, we have to prove it to him so we can get him to buy into our situation. That's what I did last time this happened to me," Maddie said that last part without realizing it would need to be explained further.

"Last time this happened to you? Maddie, you've been here before? Why didn't you say so? You must know how you got here and how to get home." Bobby was a little confused, but felt hopeful for the first time.

"No, no I was never **here** before." Maddie wasn't sure how to tell Bobby that she had traveled back in time to 1972 just a few months ago and the results of that trip were fantastic, to say the least. After all, that trip was the reason for the success of Maddie's'mores and it was also how she realized that

64

64

being popular is not the most important thing in her life. "Let's just say it's a long story and right now we have other adventures to focus on. I'll tell you all about it when we get home, if we get home! Let's look for Teddy."

Maddie and Bobby walked out of the gymnasium and into a hallway that led to a staircase that went either up or down. Maddie went down the hall a bit to see what was on this floor and found bedrooms. She thought it would be best to wait for Teddy in what looked like his room.

"All right, mother, I will do some reading and then see you in the parlor." Teddy was coming up the stairs and heading towards his room.

"Thank God you are here, Teedie. We didn't know what to do so we just came to your room. I hope that's okay." Bobby was anxious and hoped Teddy would know what to do.

"Now, Robert, please slow down. What is the trouble? I thought the two of you decided to head home when you didn't return and I had to join the family for dinner. In fact, why are you both still here?" Teddy was beginning to get annoyed by their intrusion and this worried Maddie who knew they would need his help.

"We are so sorry to bother you, Teedie. But as we said, we are not sure how we got here so we really don't know how to get home. It's not where we live that is the problem, but when we live. That's the part that we can't figure out."

Teddy was intrigued, "You have said this to me before, and I find it difficult to follow. You say you are from a different time. Do you mean to say that you have traveled in time to this very place?" Teddy asked doubtfully.

"Yes, that's exactly right. I knew you were smart and could help us figure this out. So what do you think? Can you help us travel forward in time to the year 2003 so we can get out of your hair and get home?" Bobby's enthusiasm about Teddy's help was squashed very quickly.

"I don't know what you could mean, Robert. Time travel is impossible and if you are playing some kind of a trick on me I will undoubtedly return the trick in full force. Is this something my dear friend Edith has put you up to? I must say it is quite an elaborate trick, at that."

"Look, Teedie, please understand that no one is playing a trick on you. We are really in trouble here. I know it is hard to believe but we are really from the year 2003. I don't know how it happened, but it did. Is there anything I can say to prove it to you?" Maddie pleaded.

"Well, I'm not sure. I do feel your sincerity, Maddie, and I may be starting to believe that at least this isn't a trick. Tell me again how you got to this place."

Teddy listened as Bobby and Maddie recounted the story of the argument over the book and how they were trying to save the clock from falling when they smacked heads and ended up in Teddy's living room.

"This clock you talk about is the same one that you broke today when we first met?" Teddy said thoughtfully.

"Yes, you see, Teedie, it is the same clock that

my mother bought in an antique store in New Jersey in the year 2003. I know it sounds crazy, but it shows that we traveled in time." Maddie announced feeling as if she finally proved something important. "You must believe us now."

"I do not see that the clock story proves anything of the sort. You are only telling me that your mother bought the clock that is in my home and yet there is no proof. I don't mean to call you a liar, Maddie, but in fact, it is not something you can prove. I believe in science. I need real scientific proof of your time travel. Can you show me anything that I can actually see or feel?"

Maddie and Bobby exchanged an exasperated look as they had done so many times in just this one day. Deep in thought for a few moments and listening to only the buzz of silence, Maddie finally spoke.

"Give me a minute on this one and I'm sure I can come up with something. Can I sit out on your front step, Teedie? Sometimes the fresh air helps me think."

"Of course you can. Robert and I will wait for you here. I have some reading to finish and I will find something to occupy Robert." Teddy reached for his book and suggested that Robert bring in the newspaper from the hall table. "Why not read the paper while I study?"

"Sure, why not? I'll get it and be right back." Bobby went into the hall and found the New York Herald newspaper on the table. He realized that he would be reading a newspaper from April of 1871. What would he find there? Bobby was always interested in history and did very well in school. He thought about what was happening in America in 1871 and what he would find in this paper. This is wild, Teedie, to be able to read about history on the day it happened."

"I don't know if it is wild, Robert. But you are correct. Once something happens it is history." Bobby meant something very different than Teddy, but they were both right.

Bobby was surprised by the old-fashioned look of the paper. It had very small print and was not easy to read like the papers of today that had a lot more white space and pictures. It didn't take him long to notice the front page story. "Wow, Teedie, listen to this. 'President Ulysses S. Grant signs the Ku Klux Klan Act also know as the Civil rights Act of 1871." Bobby continued reading the news story aloud. "This will not create any new civil rights but will allow for someone to take action and sue for civil rights violations. This act was prompted and passed by the U.S. Congress after the unwillingness and inability of southern lawmen to end the horrible actions of the Ku Klux Klan. Federal troops will be used to enforce this law.'" Bobby took a moment to drink it all in and try to understand what was really happening here. "Awesome. Ulysses S. Grant and Civil Rights and the whole Reconstruction thing going on after the Civil War, we studied this in social studies a few months ago and I'm reading about it as the news of the day. Can I have this paper, Teedie? No one will ever believe me but this could be the proof I need. My teacher will go nuts!" Bobby went out in the hall to tell Maddie but stopped when he saw another amazing story.

He called to Teddy, "Wait a minute. Baseball? There is a story about baseball, Teedie. Come take a look."

"Robert I have already looked at the paper and I do really need to concentrate..." Teddy's request was not heard over the ringing of excitement in Bobby's ears as he began reading the story to a frustrated Teddy.

" 'In less than a month the first professional baseball league, The National Association of Professional Baseball Players, formed right here in New York City, will play its first game at Fort Wayne. A coin flip decided the location where the Cleveland Forest Citys will meet the Fort Wayne Kekiongas for what is bound to be an exciting match. Only under-handed pitching will be permitted.' "

Bobby looked up from the paper and shook his head and laughed. "This is awesome, Teedie, baseball and history together, two of my favorite things. This is so funny about the under-handed pitching. It's only used in softball in my time. Listen to these other teams that were part of the first league: Boston Red Stockings, Chicago White Stockings, Philadelphia Athletics, and New York Mutuals. I guess it hasn't always been about the Yankees in New York, huh?"

Teddy was confused by Bobby's last statement. "Yankees have always been in New York. We **are** Yankees here in the North, Bobby. The southerners called us that all during the Civil War and even now. And before that, anyone from the New England area was called a Yankee."

"I meant the New York Yankees baseball team, Teedie. It is probably the most well-known baseball team in the history of baseball. But of course you wouldn't know that yet because the history of baseball is just starting and **I'm reading about it right now**!" Bobby's voice got louder with each word as he realized the amazing situation. "This is the coolest thing that has ever happened to me!" Bobby couldn't contain his emotions. "Teedie, I love baseball. I am going to try out for the baseball team as soon as I get back home. I was too scared to play sports before I talked to you. You see, I have asthma, too, and when I was little I had a bad attack. I have been scared it would happen again so I chose not to play any sports, and it has been pretty tough for me. My parents and other people have been trying to help me change my mind, but you were the only one who could do it. I see how you have taken control of your problems. You have no idea how you have helped me to see that it is not what happens to you in your life, but what you do about it."

"This is so true, my friend. I have found this to be the best way to live my life and the results are sure to be positive. Your choice has been to not take a chance, to not improve yourself, to not face your illness and that made you unhappy and unfulfilled. Now you have decided to take a chance, improve yourself, and face your illness. How do you feel now, Robert?"

"I feel GREAT! I have never felt better. I am going to do this! But Teedie, how can I do this in 1871. I must get back home and take control of my life."

"I will try to help you, Robert. I do believe you are from 2003. You have proven it to me by your honesty and your strong feelings. I needed to see it or feel it, and I do feel what you are telling me is true!"

Bobby had made Teddy feel the truth through his emotions and now he believed their story. But could he really help them get back to their own time?

While Bobby and Teddy were making connections about baseball, asthma, and facing problems, Maddie was on the front step outside as the sun began to sink behind the buildings. Preoccupied by her surroundings, she hadn't come up with a single idea on how to prove things to Teddy. She didn't realize that 1871 New York would look this way. In the orange glow of the sunset, horse-drawn carriages were trotting down the street. Even streetcars, also pulled by horses, carried groups of people home from work. She wasn't even sure if there was a way to get to New Jersey from New York. The tunnels weren't built yet. The bridges weren't built yet, or were they? Maddie was digging deep into her memory for anything from history class that would help her here. She made a mental note to listen more in history class; it really would come in handy and not just for time traveling.

"How can I prove that we are from the year 2003?" Maddie racked her brain. And would Teddy even be able to help them? *How would a 12-year-old boy know how to travel in time?* "If any 12-year-old boy would know what to do, it would be Teddy Roosevelt." Of that, Maddie was sure. She stayed out on the step talking to herself for a few more minutes. Maybe gazing at the clock would spark an idea. Then she turned to go inside to get the clock.

Maddie ran into the living room where the clock had been put back on the end table. It was still showing the time as 2:23. She grabbed it and took the stairs two at a time to get up to Teddy's room, but when she was only half way up the stairs she saw Bobby and Teddy at the top, excited about something. She heard Teddy say that he believed what Bobby was saying.

"You believe our story, Teedie?" Maddie said breathlessly stopping halfway up the stairway. "What made you change your mind? What was the proof?"

"Robert was the proof. He made me believe," Teddy said to Maddie from the top of the landing.

Bobby ran to meet her on the stairs. They sat on the step, and Teddy came down to join them as Bobby summarized the eye-opening events of the last few minutes. "Maddie, look at this newspaper. Read the article about the Civil Rights Act, and then read the one about the Baseball League. It's amazing to read about history in the newspaper. Stuff we read about in our text books is right here in today's newspaper. C'mon, Maddie, now you have to think history is pretty cool." Bobby was still flying high with his excitement about baseball and taking control of his life.

"This **is** totally cool, Bobby. This baseball stuff is amazing and I have to say, so is history."

"I know, but I have to get home to sign up for the team. That's what Teddy and I are so excited about," Bobby continued on excitedly, barely able to breath. "We were talking about the Yankees and how he is a Yankee and how I want to play baseball and how he helped me see that I can and that it's how you handle your problems that matters more than what your problems are and I guess he finally realized we were telling the truth." Bobby's face reddened. "And it's Theodore Roosevelt, Maddie; Theodore Roosevelt is

72

giving me advice and hanging out with us and...and..."
Bobby began to gasp for air. He couldn't seem to catch
his breath. He looked in his pocket for his inhaler, but
it wasn't there.

"Where is your inhaler, Bobby? It was in your
pocket at my house before... well before we came here."
Maddie awkwardly bent to help Bobby and lost hold
of the clock. She watched in horror as it bounced and
crashed down the staircase. It landed with a sickening
thud.

"Oh this simply can't be true. Not the clock
again. It's my favorite," Teddy cried as he pushed
past Maddie and Bobby to get to the clock. When he
approached the clock he moaned up to Maddie, "One of
the bird's heads has broken off. And there is a dent on
the right corner of the metal framing where it must have
landed. Now mother is sure to see the damage, and I
will have to take the blame for the clock and the vase."

At the same time that Teddy ran down the stairs
to retrieve the broken clock, Maddie was struggling to
help Bobby catch his breath. Finding the inhaler seemed
impossible. It was probably lost somewhere in time.

"Maddie, it's," Bobby struggled to get air
between each word, "hard -- to -- talk -- please --
help -- me."

"Try to stay calm, Bobby. I will stay right
here with you. Don't talk, just take slow easy breaths.
Maybe as you calm down it will get better." Maddie
consoled him. She wasn't sure what to say to fix the
breathing problem, so she relied on facts she was sure
of to talk Bobby through it. She talked to Bobby about
his new motivation to face his asthma and how this

73

could be the first step. She thanked him for showing her how important and yes, even interesting, history could be. She told him what a good friend he was and how much fun this adventure has been with him. She didn't know what to do to help someone with asthma. But she did know what to do to help a friend in trouble. Be there and be strong for them. She was doing that very well when they both heard Teddy describe the damage done to his favorite clock.

"Oh boy, we're in trouble now. I wrecked the clock, Bobby. But you were more important than any clock, antique or not, and I had to help you."

At that very moment in time Maddie and Bobby **both** had trouble catching their breath. Something very strange was happening, but for some reason Maddie had a smile on her face. She grabbed Bobby's hand and things went black.

Meanwhile, at the bottom of the stairs, Teddy suddenly remembered Bobby's condition and turned to offer his assistance. He was surprised to find no one there. "They must have gone to my room," Teddy said while climbing the stairs to look for them in his bedroom.

Of course, when Teddy looked in his bedroom for Maddie and Bobby, all he found was the front page of the New York Herald.

CHAPTER 11

Mrs. Morrison came running in to find Maddie and Bobby on the floor next to the history book, the table turned upside down, and books strewn on the floor. Bobby was wheezing. Maddie lay motionless next to him, eyes closed. She was still holding his hand. Mrs. Morrison quickly grabbed Bobby's inhaler, which was on the floor just next to him. "Bobby, what happened here?" She handed him the inhaler, and he took a couple of puffs and began to calm down.

He sat up. "What happened?" He answered her question with his own question. "What's wrong with Maddie? She's not getting up."

"Maddie," Mrs. Morrison shook Maddie's shoulders in alarm. "Maddie, please wake up. What is going on here?" Mrs. Morrison desperately searched the room for answers. "Bobby did you two fall, or have a fight, or I don't even know what to suggest?"

"Mom, stop shaking me. Why are you shaking me? Where is Bobby? Is he all right?" Maddie was a little woozy and unsure of her surroundings for a moment.

"Thank goodness you're okay. Let me get you a cold washcloth for your head. I'll bring you both some water and then you can tell me what in the world happened here." Despite the confusion, Bobby and Maddie realized they would need a moment to figure out what happened.

"You found your inhaler. Oh boy, I wasn't sure what to do to help you breath. I'm going to have to take a class or something. Or you're going to have to make sure you always have your inhaler."

"Or you have to make sure we don't travel in time anymore. Maybe that was the reason I couldn't breath or find my inhaler, Maddie."

"Oh wow, Bobby, you're right. What is happening? Were we really there? Teddy Roosevelt? Bobby, we met Teddy Roosevelt. Did we, really? You met him, didn't you? Or were you just in my dream? You remember it, too, don't you, Bobby?" Maddie wasn't sure for a minute if she sounded crazy or she was reminiscing with Bobby about something they both had experienced.

"Are you kidding?" Bobby didn't have a chance to finish his thought because Mrs. Morrison came back into the room, drinks in hand, and ready to hear their story.

"Bobby, I'm not kidding. You said something about time travel. You must've been there." Maddie turned to find her mother handing her a glass of water and looking at her strangely.

"Time travel, Maddie? What is all this about, honey? Maybe we should go down to the emergency room and check you both out for a concussion." Mrs. Morrison had heard Maddie tell stories before, but finding her out cold on the floor could have caused some head trauma.

"Mom, oh please, I'm fine. But I'm not sure about Bobby. How is your breathing, Bobby?" Maddie began to put the pieces together. How would she explain this to her mother? What about the clock? She rummaged around the floor for the clock. Was it still there? Did it break when it fell off the table? And, which table did she mean, hers or Teddy's? "Where is the Teddy Roosevelt clock, Mom? That's what happened. Bobby and I were kind of fighting over the *What's His Story* book and it slipped out of our hands and headed right for the clock. We both went to save it and we must've banged our heads together." She looked at Bobby with a knowing nod. This was probably what caused them to lose track of time, she realized.

Mrs. Morrison and Bobby looked around for the clock. It wasn't on the table and it wasn't in plain sight. Finally, Bobby spotted it. "There it is. It's over by the fireplace. It must've skidded across the wood floor when the book hit it."

Mrs. Morrison was the first to reach it and gasped as she went to pick it up, "Oh dear. One of the bird's heads has broken off and there is a dent in the right corner of the metal framing."

Bobby and Maddie hurried over to take a look. Maddie grabbed it from Mrs. Morrison. They looked at the clock, looked at each other, looked at the clock again, and then started jumping up and down and screaming. Bobby was the first to stop the jumping and screaming and tried to look nonchalant about the temporary giddy behavior. Maddie looked at the clock closely. "This proves we were there Bobby. The clock is the proof after all. It's exactly the same damage that Teddy described."

"Maddie, what does the clock prove, besides that you were careless. And, who is Teddy? And, I am not happy about the damage to my clock or the fact that you seem to be excited about it. I'm not happy at all!"

"Mom, you are right," Maddie realized. "The clock might have been damaged from the fall."

"Of course it was damaged from the fall. How else could it have happened? I really do think we should have you looked at. You aren't making complete sense, Maddie. I am worried about you." Mrs. Morrison was upset about her clock, but was becoming more concerned about Maddie's strange behavior.

"Mom, I am fine and Bobby is fine. I'm really sorry about the clock. I'll try to figure out how to fix this. Could we just have a minute to finish up our school stuff for this report? We only have a few days to work on it." Maddie hoped her mother would give them some time alone to debrief.

"Okay. I'll let you know when dinner is ready. Bobby, would you like to stay for dinner? I'll call your mom and let her know." Mrs. Morrison wasn't completely convinced that Maddie was 100 percent okay, but she sounded coherent, so she agreed to leave them to their school work and check on her later.

"Sure, I'll stay for dinner. Thanks, Mrs. Morrison." Bobby wanted as much time with Maddie as possible to discuss the adventure. He also just wanted to spend time with Maddie. She was fun to be with and she made him feel special. And, he never knew what might happen next with Maddie Morrison.

"This is good, Bobby. I'm glad you are staying for dinner. We'll have plenty of time to figure out what really happened here and well, you know, we'll figure out stuff." Maddie stumbled a little because her relationship with Bobby was just beginning to grow, but she already felt close to him in this short time. They had skipped some steps in the development of this friendship because of the recent unusual experience they just shared. Although, Maddie had always had a close friendship with Audrey and Julie, Bobby didn't have any close friends to rely on. This must've been a new feeling for him, to be able to confide in someone. It was hard for him to tell Maddie how thankful he was for her friendship.

"Maddie, let's talk about what we each think happened and I'll write some things down. We need to keep track of this information. We can probably use some of it in our report for Mrs. Brenner's class." They began at the beginning, talking about the moment they arrived in Teddy's living room, the clock, the gymnasium visit, and Teddy's motivating speech on controlling asthma. Then they remembered: the facts they had decided not to tell Teddy, the worry about getting home, the newspaper headlines, Teddy believing their story, and finally the clock falling down Teddy's staircase. They were in agreement on everything. It had all happened just as they thought. How was this possible?

"So it wasn't a dream? We were there. I'm sure we didn't say anything to change the course of Teddy's life. He was pretty amazing though. I mean c'mon, the way he talked first of all, and the way he did things for himself. He is the same age as us, Bobby. Our parents usually have to remind us to do the things that are "good" for us. He did it all himself. He knew that when his parents told him it was the right thing, that it was the right thing. He didn't question them, he trusted their judgment. He saw a problem and he did what he had to do to fix it."

"That's it, Maddie. That's where we start our report, showing Teddy as a boy with the characteristics of a reformer, changing things for the better. Look what he did with his asthma problem. He changed himself into a strong, healthy boy. I'm going to do it, too. I'm going to ask my mom to sign me up for baseball tomorrow. The games have just started I think, so I hope I can still get on a team."

"You'll make it happen. I have no doubt. You have that motivation and determination to make things better, just like Teddy."

"Well, now I think I do, Maddie. This has to be the coolest thing that has ever happened to me in my whole life!" Bobby turned to face Maddie and asked her, "How about you, Maddie, coolest thing ever or what?"

"Let me think." Maddie was considering another time travel adventure she recently took and also the invention of s'mores and before too much time passed Bobby broke into her thoughts.

"Are you serious? What could be cooler than meeting Teddy Roosevelt, our 26th president, as a 12-year-old, in 1871! It's not even something I would have ever thought about in my wildest imagination. You can't possibly have done anything better than this."

"Of course, you're right, Bobby. I was just thinking about, well it doesn't matter. We have quite a story to tell. But wait a minute. No one will ever believe it. Should we even tell anyone?" Maddie wondered aloud.

"Maybe we shouldn't," Bobby said thoughtfully. "Everyone will think we're nuts. Let's keep it to ourselves for a while. Maybe we can tell Mrs. Brenner. She would love this whole story."

"Bobby, the only problem with your idea is that I don't think Mrs. Brenner is going to believe us either. Just because she's a history teacher and would be interested in this stuff, doesn't mean she'll believe this crazy story." Maddie was right of course. They decided to use the adventure to make their report on Teddy Roosevelt as good as it could be. Using the idea of him as a boy reformer was agreed upon and it made for a great start to their report.

"Maddie, I like what we have so far, but I think we need to do some more research. Meeting Teddy as a boy did not give us any information about the things he did as president and the reforms we have to write about."

"Okay. Let's eat dinner and then we will do some research on the computer and use the book my dad gave me." Maddie couldn't believe she had to do research when she had actually met the man she was reporting on. She realized they had more to learn and was actually looking forward to finding things about Teddy Roosevelt as a man. So she took one more quick look in the *What's His Story* book before going in for dinner. "HUH? Oh no, this is impossible! I know this

wasn't here when I looked at the book earlier. Bobby!"
Maddie called quietly and when he didn't answer she
yelled louder, "BOBBY, BOBBY! Come in here. This
you won't believe."

CHAPTER 12

"What is it, Maddie? Your mom has dinner on the table and we are waiting for you." Bobby leaned into the room and noticed Maddie staring and pointing at a page in the book. "What? You want me to read it?" Bobby had to read the signals she was sending because Maddie was speechless. Bobby read the passage she was pointing to.

" 'When the young Roosevelt was about 12 years old he took control of his weakened condition and began physical training to strengthen his body. Not only did Teddy Roosevelt help himself, but he felt especially proud of passing on his determination to others with the same medical condition. He continued to work at being a strong man physically and mentally throughout his life.' "

"Well?" Maddie said as she gestured at the book.

"Well, what?" Bobby answered not knowing what was troubling Maddie.

"That line was not there before," Maddie snapped in a frustrated voice.

"What line?" Bobby questioned as he looked over the passage again.

"This one. Right here, Bobby!" Maddie read it

out loud with feeling.

" 'Not only did Teddy Roosevelt help himself, but he felt especially proud of passing on his determination to others with the same medical condition.' "

"I know it wasn't in there before. I'm sure of it. And now it is. They are talking about you. How he passed on the determination to "**others**" with the same medical condition. Teddy must've told someone about us for it to become part of his story. He knew us, Bobby, and he cared. We were really there!" Maddie flung herself on the couch and cupped her hands over her face as she writhed around in amazement.

Bobby grabbed the book and read the passage over and over again. He had only seen it for a brief time when he came over to Maddie's house after school earlier today. She read it to him when he was looking for insight as to how Teddy Roosevelt had overcome his asthma. Bobby remembered that, but he couldn't be sure of the exact words in the book. It was pretty spooky how much it connected to their experience.

"I think you might be right. What else could it mean? Now I really have to face my fears and take control of my life. Teddy would be disappointed in me if I didn't." Bobby declared. "C'mon, Maddie, let's go eat and then I can go home and talk to my parents about the baseball sign-ups. We can work on the report tomorrow in school and I'll come over again, if that's okay."

"Sure, okay, Bobby. Let's eat and take a break from all this Teddy Roosevelt stuff. It's a little too much for me anyway. We'll sleep on it and talk more tomorrow." Maddie's head was spinning from the slight change in the book that seemed to have taken place as a result of their time travel. She had been careful not to divulge any information that might change the course of history while they were visitors in the past. Maddie felt confident that there wouldn't be any more surprises. They could just enjoy the awesome memory and the effects it had on them. She wondered if she should keep this from Audrey and Julie. Her friends loved being entertained by her stories, but they would never believe this one.

The next morning Maddie got ready for school but something was different. She was looking forward to going. She wondered what Mrs. Brenner might tell them about Teddy Roosevelt and for that matter, anything about history. It all seemed more real to her somehow. It all made more sense and had something to do with her for the first time ever.

Dad was right about history being interesting and all, Maddie admitted to herself. *I guess parents do know the right things a lot of the time.*

Breakfast was waiting for her, but she just gulped down a little orange juice and grabbed a piece of cinnamon toast and was out the door in a flash. Her mother didn't even have a chance to see her and only yelled from the laundry room to remember her lunch money on the counter.

Audrey and Maddie both arrived to school at the same time. Their bus routes always seemed to arrive simultaneously. They had begun to rely on this timing and would meet up at the front door of school each morning.

"Maddie," Audrey called from the sidewalk as she approached the front door, "why didn't you call me last night and let me know how things went with Bobby? Was he nice to you? Did you get along? How is the report coming? Is he as cute as we thought, you know, close up and all?"

"Audrey, stop asking so many questions. I can't even remember any except the last one. So I can answer that one for you. Yes, he is definitely as cute as we thought, close up and far away." How would Maddie explain their sudden close relationship? It was going to be obvious that Bobby and she had developed a friendship that would normally take longer than spending one afternoon together. Maddie decided not to worry about that, but instead she'd focus on the positive things that would come from the time travel adventure with Bobby. Just as she made that decision, one of the positive results came walking toward her with a smile.

"Hey, Maddie," Bobby said as he gave her a nudge in her side, "what's new?"

"What's new with you is the question. Did you talk to your parents about signing up for baseball?" Maddie asked with a genuine interest. "Tell me the whole story."

Audrey was listening to the conversation and was surprised that one afternoon with Maddie had helped Bobby to change his whole attitude about playing sports. She knew Maddie could be persuasive, but this was quite an accomplishment. She heard Bobby tell Maddie that he was signing up for baseball today at the rec center. Audrey followed Maddie and

Bobby to their lockers and was unnoticed as they talked about baseball sign ups, their Teddy Roosevelt report, and their plan to work on it at Maddie's after school today.

"Maddie," Audrey interrupted causing both Maddie and Bobby to notice her for the first time, "I thought we were going to hang out after school today?"

"I really can't, Audrey. Bobby and I are on a roll with this report for social studies and we want to pick up where we left off yesterday. He won't even get to my house til around 4:00 because he is signing up for baseball first. Isn't that great, Audrey? Why don't you come over tomorrow after school and we can hang out then and talk about stuff." Maddie didn't want to cause any suspicion and she didn't want to make Audrey feel bad. How would she juggle this time travel secret and her new friendship with Bobby and still keep her friendship with Audrey strong. Past experience has shown that keeping secrets from Audrey is not easy to do.

I am going to have to tell Audrey. And, why shouldn't I? She will love this story and then all three of us can be close. I don't like keeping Audrey on the outside of anything. I'm already lying to her. Maddie thought to herself that if anyone would believe the story, it would be Audrey. Her decision was made. Audrey would be the first to know. Maddie would tell her the whole story tomorrow. But Maddie already had another idea of how to tell everyone without really telling anyone.

As Maddie walked into social studies class, she felt the excitement. She was an insider now. She was a part of history. It all seemed so much more important. Mrs. Brenner went over the requirements for the president report, reminded them that the report was due on Thursday, and gave the class time to work in their pairs.

"How are you two doing with Teddy Roosevelt?" Maddie and Bobby looked up as Mrs. Brenner asked about their progress. "There are plenty of things that he did to help America. It may help you to find out his motivation for some of his reforms. Finding out about the man behind the president will add some interest for you and for us as you present your report." Mrs. Brenner was hoping to spark an interest in the people of history for her students.

"We have already done that, Mrs. Brenner," Maddie blurted out with excitement. "We know all about Teddy Roosevelt as a boy. Did you know they called him Teedie when he was younger? Did you know that he had asthma and did exercises to get strong?"

Mrs. Brenner smiled and jumped in to comment, "I love these facts, Maddie, and it sounds like you have more, and I am impressed with your enthusiasm. Talk to me about what you two are planning to do with this important information about TR as a boy?"

"Well, we thought we would show how Teddy Roosevelt was a reformer from the time he was a young boy," Bobby continued, "making things better for himself and nature. We found out about his interest in nature and his family's part in the Museum of Natural History in New York." Bobby was proud of the idea and was looking for his teacher's approval.

He got it. "I love this idea, Bobby. You two have done an amazing amount of research in just one afternoon. Good for you. Let me suggest that you look into Teddy's reforms and accomplishments as president and make the connections to his boyhood dreams and hobbies. I can't wait to see how you put all this into a creative presentation." Mrs. Brenner looked forward to seeing all her students' final presentations. But although Bobby had done well in class, he, and especially Maddie, had not shown this kind of enthusiasm in the past. Their project had special interest for her.

"It's going to be some kind of look-back-in-the-past kind of thing," Maddie explained. She hadn't really discussed her idea with Bobby yet, but she had a feeling he would agree with it. "We haven't put it all together, but I think you will like it, Mrs. Brenner."

Maddie had been thinking about their presentation all day and couldn't wait to tell Bobby. When the teacher walked away she turned to Bobby, "Bobby, let's do a skit or something where we travel back in time and meet Teddy Roosevelt and find out all the stuff we found out and it will be our way of telling everyone, but not really telling anyone," Maddie spewed out the whole idea in one breath and hoped Bobby would like it.

"It's just what I was thinking. I swear it's been on my mind all day and I couldn't wait to talk to **you** about it. We just have to figure out how to put in the information about the presidential years and what he did with all his ideas from when he was a boy. This is going to be very cool and fun, even."

Bobby and Mrs. Gordon showed up at Maddie's house at 4:00. "Hi, Mrs. Gordon, my mom is in the kitchen cooking, or baking, or something. Did Bobby sign up for baseball?"

"He sure did!" Mrs. Gordon beamed at Bobby with pride. She was so relieved to see Bobby's new attitude about his asthma and would do anything to help support his new excitement over sports. "He starts practice tomorrow with the town league and he was put on a team with some boys from your class."

"Yeah, Maddie, this is going to be great. You know Dylan, Joey, and Ben. All three of them are on my team. I'll be a little tied up with practice so we have to get right to work on our project and maybe meet at night instead of after school tomorrow." Bobby was very responsible for a 12-year-old boy and wanted to keep up his school work along with his new baseball schedule.

"We can meet whenever you want, Bobby. I'm sure my mom can bring me to your house if that is easier. The report is due in a couple of days anyway and we might finish today, so we won't have to worry about setting up meetings after that." Maddie suddenly realized that she would have to find another reason to hang out with him after this report was finished.

Bobby's mom went into the kitchen to catch up with Mrs. Morrison, and the kids got right down to work. "Look, Bobby, it is still there. The line is still in the book. I didn't know if I was just dreaming, but it is really there."

"We were really there. I'm sure of it, Maddie. This is the proof. What about the damage on the clock?

Don't you think that is weird, too?" Maddie and Bobby spent a few minutes convincing each other that their time travel adventure did really happen. It was still a little hard to believe, even for them. How would they make anyone else believe it? Maybe they didn't have to make anyone believe it. But Maddie and Bobby were going to tell their story!

CHAPTER 13

"Okay, so how do you like my idea?" Maddie explained her idea of how to present the story as their class report. "If we do it this way, we get to tell our story and we will also show how creative and smart we are at the same time. I'll be the teacher in the skit and explain to the class about this new technology that I have purchased for the classroom. It is a time travel machine that will let us all be spectators to history. Traveling through time can cause problems, however, if you interact with anyone or anything. With this in mind, we will only be able to watch and listen to whomever and whatever we want," Maddie said acting like a teacher would. She went on in her teacher voice. "Now class, we will be visiting Teddy Roosevelt as a 12-year-old, in the year 1871, to learn about the boy behind the man."

"This is totally great, Maddie, and I'll be Teddy Roosevelt as a boy. The class can watch me...let me think, look at birds, maybe, exercise, studying or something. I think we should also show how he does all this stuff without his parents telling him to."

They brainstormed ideas on how to show that Teddy was motivated about his own intelligence, health, and nature. They were sure to add facts about the Museum of Natural History and the news stories of the time. They started writing the script they would use for their classroom presentation. It wasn't hard at all. They just wrote what actually happened to them. The next step was researching the presidential reforms accomplished by Theodore Roosevelt. When they discovered that he was the first president to focus on conservation of natural resources and create national parks, they knew he followed through on his boyhood beliefs. Cleaning up cities, factories, and corrupt businesses with his strong hand and good heart confirmed that the boy that they had met became a man who stuck to his principles and made things happen. They had the time travel machine move ahead to 1906, during Roosevelt's presidency, to present the new-found information about his reforms. They wrote original lines for this part. They still didn't have much trouble because they felt as if they knew the man.

"I love it!" Maddie squealed as she put the finishing touches on her closing statements for the skit. They put stage directions in their script so the kids in class would feel as if they were actually traveling through time. They also wrote in lines for some of them to say. "Since I'm playing the teacher, I can teach the class something in this role, if only for a moment. I want to say something about how we feel, Bobby, since it happened to us. Can we make other kids get the feeling just by making believe they're experiencing it? Something about how these presidents and history guys were once kids like us and there is a story behind all the things we study. Wait, I have an idea. Let's call our skit "What's His Story?" You know, like the book my dad gave me."

"Yes, it's good. I think it will help some kids get the idea. I like how we wrote my part as Teddy. He is a good kid and we made him fun and interesting. I think our friends will like him. Who would have ever thought of any of our presidents as 12-year-olds? It makes it all make more sense to me."

"You know what makes sense to me? We are almost finished with our project and it was fun to do. I actually had fun doing school work. This **is** really good stuff! Okay, I'll type it up, Bobby, and bring you a copy to look over tomorrow. We'll make copies for the class so they can say their lines, you know like "ooh" and "ahh," in all the right places. And, well, that's it, right? So, I guess we won't have to meet after school anymore," Maddie sighed.

Bobby had just the answer she was hoping for. "We don't have to meet for school, but we can still meet for fun."

"This actually was fun, Bobby. But if we don't have something to work on for school, we can just hang out and watch TV or something, right?" Maddie said waiting for Bobby to agree.

"Sure, I guess so. I'll probably have to go to practice and all, but maybe you can come to that sometime. And remember, you promised to be there at my games to cheer me on. We will definitely see each other, Maddie."

They were both sure they wanted to see each other and knew they had a special bond. Maddie's worries over how they would meet up again wouldn't last too long. Maddie thought about how quickly her friendship grew with Julie over the last few months. When she and Audrey invited her over to sit at their lunch table one day in school it was friend at first sight. They just clicked immediately. They almost heard the click in the air and from then on it was Maddie, Audrey, and Julie laughing, making s'mores, and confiding their deepest thoughts to each other. Now maybe Bobby would join in the fun. Somehow having a boy as a friend would put a different spin on things. Maddie couldn't wait to see Audrey and Julie and discuss the possibilities.

The next day in school Maddie waited by the front door for Audrey and grabbed her arm as they pushed through the front door together.

"Let's find Julie because I want to talk to you guys about Bobby."

"What about Bobby? Is he okay? Did he sign up for baseball? Did you have a problem with your social studies project? Are you going on a date or something?" Audrey spouted out her usual deluge of questions and Maddie gave her the usual response.

"Stop asking me so many questions, Audrey. I can only remember the last one anyway," she laughed. "No, Bobby and I are not going on a date, but we are going to be very good friends for sure. That's what I want to talk to you about."

Maddie searched the halls for Julie and swirled Audrey around when she saw her coming around the corner. "Julie," she called as she pulled Audrey with her towards Julie's locker. "Bobby Gordon and I have been hanging around together the past few days. But it's weird because it seems like weeks and since my parents and his parents are really good friends, it seems like years almost, and so I just want you both to know that we are really good friends now and he is gonna be like, you know, one of us. You know what I mean." Just then an eighth grade boy bumped into Maddie knocking her books to the floor. Without even missing a beat, she bent down to pick up her books and continued babbling. Audrey and Julie crouched down not wanting to miss any juicy details and helped Maddie retrieve her books. "He's so nice and I think we will all have so much fun hanging out with him. You have to come with me to his baseball games. Dylan, Ben, and Joey are on his team, so this could be very cool. So what do you think?" Maddie had to take a very deep breath after that long speech and then she waited for their answer as she let her breath out. She looked at them. Audrey and Julie eyed each other and then burst out laughing. They weren't sure if they were laughing at her story or the fact that Maddie had just dropped all her books again.

"Of course, Bobby can be one of us. We can always use some good friends and he sounds like a good one." Audrey handed Maddie one last book left on the ground. "Baseball games sound good, too."

"I don't think sleep-overs will work, but we can have him over to taste our s'mores creations and stuff," Julie giggled.

They were good friends and knew Maddie well enough to know that if she thought Bobby was a good person, they would think so too.

"Oh, hey, Maddie, Mr. Rivers said we were coming into your class to watch you do your president presentations. And, Audrey, he said that your class is coming too."

"Oh yeah, I keep forgetting to tell you, Maddie. Isn't that cool? Are you and Bobby working on something good?" Audrey asked.

"Oh this is better than I thought with you two there. You will love the idea we came up with. I'm not going to tell you though. You won't believe how great it is." Maddie was so glad that her best friends would hear the whole adventure. They actually might believe how great it is, but Maddie wondered if they would ever believe how real it was.

Audrey came over after school that day just like they had arranged. Maddie started to wonder if she should tell Audrey the story now as she had planned or just let her enjoy the presentation in class tomorrow. Since Audrey was her closest friend, they always confided in each other. *This shouldn't be any different. Good friends need to know they can tell each other things that mean a lot whether they are silly, or special, or sometimes hard to believe.* Maddie decided to confide in Audrey and tell her the story before telling the whole class. The class would just think it was pretty cool, but Audrey would know it was true. That was the difference with a good friend, they know the inside story.

"Okay, Audrey, get in here and sit down. I have a story to tell you," Maddie ordered as she pulled Audrey in the front door.

"What is it? Does it have to do with Bobby? Do you feel okay? Are you moving or something terrible? Did your mom make a new s'mores recipe? What is the story, Maddie?"

Audrey's questions came much too fast, as always. Maddie answered the only one that really mattered. "Audrey, stop talking for one moment and I will tell you the story. It's amazing, really, and I want you to be the first to hear it. I don't even know how to begin. You probably won't believe it and **I** almost don't believe it, except that I was there and I actually have proof. Some people might not think it was proof, but it is proof, I'm sure of it. It wasn't in the book before we went and the clock was broken in the exact same places and I just know it happened," Maddie insisted.

"Okay, Maddie, I have no clue what you are talking about. What proof? Do you mean the Teddy Roosevelt clock that your mom just bought? She must be so mad that it's broken. Is that the story? You broke the clock?"

"No, it's not the story. But, yes I broke the clock. But it wasn't in the house here when I broke it. It was in Teddy Roosevelt's house and we were there in his house. That's the story."

"You were in Teddy Roosevelt's house? What are you talking about?" Audrey had heard Maddie tell some crazy stories before so she was ready for anything, or so she thought.

"We both were. Bobby and I were there together. It happened kind of quickly when we were fighting over the book my dad gave me. Bobby wanted to see how Teddy took control of his asthma and that's when he admitted to me that he had asthma. My mom had told me about an asthma attack that scared him when he was younger. This was the reason he wasn't playing sports. So, anyway, he got really excited and out of breath and we lost hold of the book and it went flying across the room. It hit the clock and it fell and we tried to catch it and banged heads and woke up in Teddy's house in 1871. He was our age, Audrey. It was so cool." Maddie went on to tell Audrey everything that happened during their time with Teddy. She recalled each moment vividly. She went on to explain how Bobby was motivated by Teddy and his struggle to overcome his asthma. "That's why he signed up for baseball. That's why he feels so good about himself and the possibilities. And the whole experience made me pretty excited about history. It's weird how different I feel, Audrey. I'm so happy for Bobby and I'm happy for me, too. And now I'm even happier because you know and I can share it all with you!"

"WOW! Wow! Okay so you traveled in time. Are you sure it wasn't just a dream? You did bang heads. Maybe you blacked out." It's not that Audrey didn't believe Maddie; she was just trying to make sense of it all.

"No we didn't black out or have a dream. We were totally there having the same experience. How could that happen? Oh and look here is the proof." Maddie showed Audrey the newly added line in the book and the damage to the clock that was the same damage when it fell down the stairs in Teddy's house.

Audrey took the book and read silently. She touched the jagged edges of the clock thoughtfully. "I can't remember if this line had been in the book before. And the damage to the clock could've happened when it fell off the table right here in your own house.

You know, when the book hit it." Audrey was being realistic, as much as she wanted to believe Maddie's improbable story.

"You don't believe me, Audrey? I know it sounds crazy, but you're my best friend. How could you not believe me? I am not lying to you. It really happened just like I told you." Maddie felt betrayed. She had looked forward to sharing her story with Audrey, thinking she would join in her excitement. It hadn't occurred to her that she wouldn't believe her at all. She was beginning to get angry. "Why don't you believe me? Are you mad because Bobby was with me and not you? I didn't have any control over that. If I had a choice I would've loved to have had you with me."

"Maddie, please don't get mad at me. I don't think you are lying at all. I love this story and yes, I guess I would've loved to have been there with you. But don't **you** think it would be hard for someone to believe?" Audrey didn't want to make Maddie feel bad. "I do know that something amazing happened to you. I have never seen you this excited about school, and you really know so much about Teddy Roosevelt. You have made me want to find out more about him and other presidents. And come to think of it, Bobby did change his attitude about his asthma and getting involved in sports pretty fast. I guess it kind of makes sense." Audrey said doubtfully trying her hardest to believe it.

"So you do believe me? I knew you would. You are my best friend, Audrey. And somehow it all didn't seem as real until I told you." Maddie realized.

"Sometimes I don't know what to expect next

from you, Maddie. But it's always something fun. I love being your best friend, Maddie Morrison." Audrey hugged her tightly but still wondered if there would ever be an explanation for this story. *I guess it really doesn't matter,* Audrey thought. *Things are always more real when you share it with a friend.*

CHAPTER 14

"Mom, can I bring Teddy's clock to school for my presentation today?" Maddie wanted to use the clock to add reality to their time travel skit. "I promise to be extra careful. I'm sure Mrs. Brenner will hold onto it for me for the day so it will be safe."

"I don't know, Maddie. It's broken and I was going to bring it back to the antique store to see if they could recommend a place that could repair a piece like this."

"Mom, it's just for this one day. I'll bring it home this afternoon. Please, Mom, it will make the skit so much better and I'll be real careful."

"All right, honey. You have to be careful with it even though it is already broken. I'm not going to the antique mall until Saturday, anyway. Just be careful and bring it right home," Mrs. Morrison reminded her again.

"Mom, I promise I will be **so** careful. I know how important the clock is to you. I feel really bad that I broke it. I will bring it right home after school. I can really be responsible." Maddie wanted her mom to trust her with this responsibility. She had learned from Teddy the importance of listening to your parents.

"Okay, I do believe that you will take good care

of it." Mrs. Morrison could hear a change in Maddie's voice: a new found responsibility and attention to what she was being told. "I guess you have been listening to me after all. I'll try not to repeat myself," she said giving Maddie's face a loving squeeze. She knew this would be a hard habit to break.

"Believe me, Mom. I hear you and I'm learning to listen even more! I love you." Maddie gave her mom a kiss, grabbed a soda, and headed for the family room to watch some TV.

"I'm glad you're my daughter, Maddie Morrison. I love you, too, and did you know I also like you very much?" Mrs. Morrison felt her daughter growing up right before her eyes.

Maddie held the clock tightly as she arrived at her locker that morning. Bobby came up behind her and tapped on her the right shoulder but then ducked to her left. She swirled her head around to the right then to the left and made a face at Bobby.

"Very funny, Bobby, I'm trying to concentrate on the clock here. Could you hold it for a minute while I put this other stuff in my locker? I want to bring it right to Mrs. Brenner so she can hold onto it for the day until we present later on."

"Sure. I can't believe your mom let you bring it. Wasn't she worried that you might break it again?"

"Yes, but I convinced her that I would be really careful and that it was key for our presentation. It will totally add a realistic touch to a fantastic story. I wonder if anyone will believe that time travel is even possible. Anyway, I just hope Mrs. Brenner thinks it's good." Maddie was excited and hopeful that she would get a good grade on this and bring her social studies average up. After all, she had been hovering around a C all marking period.

"I think she will definitely like it and we will probably get an A. This is the best thing I have ever done in social studies, and I have been getting mostly A's and some B's. We make a good team, Maddie. And it doesn't hurt that one of our team members was the man, or should I say the boy himself, Teddy Roosevelt."

"I told Audrey everything. She didn't believe me at first, but then I think she did. Kind of the same way that Teddy believed you. You know, because of how strong our feelings were. Audrey saw something different about me and even you, so she had no other explanation. And why would I lie?" Maddie reasoned.

"That's cool. Listen, I have to go to homeroom and I want to look over the script a little. Do you have the copies for the class? This is going to be so great. I'll see you later."

"Okay, Bobby, and yes I made all the copies and everything is all set." He walked down the hall and gave her a thumbs up.

Audrey, Julie, and Maddie met up for lunch as they did every day. Audrey gave Maddie a hug when she saw her.

"What was that for?" Maddie wondered as she smiled at Audrey.

"I don't even know. I just felt like giving you a hug. I'm so glad you told me your story yesterday. It will make your presentation today that much better for me."

After the girls shared their fries, cookies, and

ice cream they decided they would get together over the week-end for a movie or something fun. "Maybe we'll invite Bobby, too," Maddie offered.

"Oh yeah, that would be very cool and maybe he'll bring some of the other guys and we can hang out and stuff." Julie agreed and Audrey nodded as they all giggled with anticipation of the fun times ahead. "Well, I'll see you both in social studies. Good luck, Maddie."

"Thanks, Julie. See you guys later. And don't make me laugh or anything, I really want to do well on this." Maddie added as she threw out the cookie wrapper, making her think of a new s'mores idea for her mom. She would try to remember it and tell her mom later. Right now, the only thing she wanted to think about was her Teddy Roosevelt time travel skit.

"This is it, Bobby. Should we tell Mrs. Brenner that we want to go first? I want to make sure we get to go today because I have to bring the clock home. I promised my mom."

"Yeah, go tell her. We're ready." Bobby felt as excited as Maddie. There had been so many changes as a result of meeting Teddy Roosevelt. It was a feeling that he didn't want to lose, and Bobby was pretty sure he would feel this good for a long time.

The students from the other two classes began to arrive and crowded around the back of the room. Some found seats on the window sill. Still others squished next to their friends on a single desk chair. The noise level rose as students talked excitedly. Mrs. Brenner let Maddie and Bobby go first. Bobby passed out the scripts to their classmates. Maddie and Bobby set up some desks in the front and used Mrs. Brenner's chair for the Teddy scenes. They set the clock on a table next to the chair.

They began. Suddenly the room went quiet. Their dramatic presentation along with the content and the time travel idea pulled everyone in. They had chosen a helper to flash the lights just at the time the class was traveling back in time. This added to the suspenseful atmosphere that was building in the classroom. Even the teachers in the room were intrigued. The few students that were given some dialogue played their parts perfectly. The "oohs" and "aahs" came at just the right moments as the class followed along in their scripts. They watched the skit without any other sounds. It was going better than Maddie had hoped. The facts were good, too. Maddie and Bobby emphasized the reforms at all the right places so they were sure to do everything the teacher asked for to receive a good grade. It was time to return to the present and the helper flashed the lights again and Maddie announced to the class, still in character, "Our time travel device has given you the chance to see history happening before your very eyes. This is something you should never forget. As young people today you must always remember that history is made up of people who were once boys and girls, just like you. You can also do wonderful things if you put your mind and heart into it as Teddy Roosevelt did. History is his story, her story, and your story. Make yours a good one and you can make history, too."

No one said anything. It was quiet and Maddie and Bobby waited anxiously. Mrs. Brenner walked to the front of the room and the class seemed to be deep in thought. There wasn't a sound for what seemed like a few minutes. Mrs. Brenner took advantage of the silence. She was aware that the students were affected by the presentation as was she; she let them think for a moment. Maddie and Bobby weren't sure what to think, but Mrs. Brenner was quite sure what was going on here.

"Let me say that I have never seen my class so involved in a presentation before. I have never seen my class so affected by a presentation before. I, myself, was drawn in and felt like I was there with you. Maddie and Bobby you two have done something that is very difficult to do. You made history come alive for us and you made it real. Thank-you and I think the class wants to thank-you, too." Mrs. Brenner motioned to the students to show their appreciation.

It took a split second for the class to snap out of their thoughts and then the clapping started. First it was slow, then it was a full applause, and then there were some hoots and hollers and even a few whistles. Maddie and Bobby couldn't stop smiling. Maddie caught Audrey's eye and was rewarded with her friend's awed expression. Audrey's eyes glistened with pride. They had told their story and everyone loved it. But best of all everyone believed it. They had made history real and Maddie felt like she had made a difference.

CHAPTER 15

Maddie rushed in the door after school and ran right to the table to put the clock back gently. No one was home yet. She remembered that her mom had an important meeting that afternoon. She and Denise were presenting a whole new line of s'mores flavors to the distributor. Maddie touched the clock. She smoothed her finger over the dent in the right corner as her thoughts turned to the events of this past week. *Was it really only last Saturday that Mom had bought the clock and Dad had given me the book? It felt more like 100 years had passed not just a few days.* Maddie would never forget this week and knew that it had made a big difference in her life.

"Maddie, I'm home," Mrs. Morrison announced as she came through the side door. "What a great meeting today. They loved the new flavors. Double Chocolate Chip S'mores, Toasted Coconut S'mores, Maple Walnut S'mores and most of all, your creation: Sundae Surprise S'mores. It really was everyone's favorite. Maddie you are a genius. Speaking of being a genius," Mrs. Morrison added, "how did your presentation go at school today? Did the clock help? How did Bobby do? Tell me everything."

By now Mrs. Morrison had found her way into the family room where Maddie's smile gave away her answer. "You have no idea how great we were. We were great, Mom. Bobby and I did it just like we planned. The kids in class followed the lines perfectly and the teacher loved it. She said we made history come alive for everyone. We made it all real!" Maddie gushed with excitement and pride.

"Honey, that is fantastic. I want all the details. Come in the kitchen with me and let's make something special for dinner to celebrate. What would you like?"

"Anything is good. I love everything you make, Mom. And tell me more about the s'mores meeting. They really liked my idea the best?" Maddie and her mom talked all the way into the kitchen and all through the preparations for a celebration dinner. They even planned to go to the antique mall together on Saturday to see about fixing the clock. When Mr. Morrison came home he heard happy sounds from the kitchen and the house smelled delicious.

"It sounds and smells like things are going very well for my girls. What's for dinner? And what has you two so giddy?" Phil Morrison came home from work many times to hear laughter and to smell good food, but somehow there was an atmosphere of excitement today.

Maddie was the first to greet her dad. "This is a celebration dinner, Dad. Bobby and I did really great on our presentation today. Mom's new s'mores flavors were a big hit, too. They loved my s'mores flavor the most." She nudged her mom and giggled. "Go wash up for dinner, Dad, and meet us back here for the rest of the story. I have a lot to thank-you for, too."

"Well, I am looking forward to this for sure. I can't wait to hear how **I** contributed to this success story. I'll be right down. Save me a seat, girls." Mr. Morrison was curious to hear all the details, but most of all, he loved seeing Maddie so happy.

"They were silent when we finished," Maddie said remembering the feeling she had in the moments following the presentation. "We weren't sure what to think, at first. We thought we had done a good job, but nothing happened. Finally, Mrs. Brenner announced how well we had done and how we made history real for the class. She said it is very hard to do. She loved it, Dad. I'm pretty sure I got an A. But I am definitely sure that you helped me to get excited about it all with the book you gave me. Thanks, Dad." Maddie gave her dad a hug.

"You like the book, Maddie. I'm so glad. I can see that you are going to enjoy social studies more and we will have something to talk about. There's nothing more important to me than you, Maddie. This is all great news. I'm very happy and very proud of you." Mr. Morrison smiled and kept smiling for the rest of the meal.

Maddie felt good about how her dad felt. She glowed thinking about the positive consequences of her trip back in time. Her dad was happy that she liked the book. He was glad she found history interesting. He wasn't gloating and saying things like, I told you so, or I knew I was right, or if only you had listened to me sooner. He was just happy for her. It made it easy for Maddie to declare, "You were right, Dad. History

110

is pretty cool and I do feel a connection to it from the book and well, just getting to know the characters and all." Maddie knew her dad would love the Teddy story, but for now things were perfect the way they were. She would know when it was the right time to tell **"her story**."

The next day in school Maddie and Bobby couldn't wait to get to social studies and get their grade on the project. Bobby described how well baseball practice was going in just these two days and that he was hoping to play in the game on Saturday afternoon. Maddie said she would be there and hopefully Audrey and Julie would be able to go, too.

Throughout the day, kids came up to them and said what a great report they did. They had a good day but still wondered what their grade would be as they entered Mrs. Brenner's class.

Maddie was talking to Bobby as they walked in the room. "I can't wait to see you play baseball. Are you excited? What time does it start? Oh wait a minute. She is handing out the grades. Do you think we got an A? I am almost positive we got an A. What do you think?"

Maddie didn't have to wait for Bobby to answer because Mrs. Brenner put the grade on their desks and said, "You two did a fine job and it was obvious how much effort you put into your presentation." Bobby grabbed it and looked first and turned to Maddie. "We didn't get an A, Maddie."

"What? We had to get an A. She said how good we did and everything," Maddie stopped speaking as Bobby showed her the paper. "A+, oh my gosh!

A+, Bobby, we got an A+. We are amazing. Teddy is amazing. Good old Teedie!" They gave each other a knowing look and Maddie liked this feeling: doing well in school. Maddie and Bobby were rewarded for their hard work and the A+ was only one of those rewards.

CHAPTER 16

Maddie rubbed the sleep from her eyes, yawned, and smiled to herself. Saturday! She loved Saturdays because there was so much to do, especially today. Today was Bobby's first baseball game. She was going to see the results of her "reforms." Changing things for the better was exactly what Maddie Morrison always tried to do. It sure felt good to see the changes in Bobby Gordon since he started playing baseball. He was so happy doing what he loves. Before going to the game, Maddie and her mom would be stopping at the antique mall to see about getting the clock fixed. Mrs. Morrison was surprised but happy that Maddie wanted to go with her. Maddie had a new appreciation for the antique mall since she had done some antiquing of her own, so to speak. The main reason she wanted to go was to see the end table at the store where her mother had bought the clock. Maddie tried to remember the one in Teddy's house. She was hoping the table at the store might be the same one that Teddy bumped into when they first surprised him at his house.

"Mom, I'm ready to go. C'mon, we have to be back in time to make Bobby's game at 2:00. Are you going to go with me? I told Audrey and Julie we would pick them up. You should stay with us. I'm sure Mrs.

Gordon will be there," Maddie was babbling on as Mrs. Morrison came into the room and gave Maddie a look of surprise.

"You **are** ready! I am a little surprised. I think this is the first time, yes, it is definitely the first time you have been ready and waiting for me. I like it, Maddie. This is definitely a change for the better, my little reformer. Let's go." Mrs. Morrison had the clock in one hand and took Maddie's arm with the other and led her out to the car.

"So, do you think they'll be able to fix the clock, Mom?"

"I hope so. And to answer your question from before, yes, I think I will stay at Bobby's game. This is so great that he is playing ball. I'm happy for him and his parents. They are so relieved that he has changed his attitude. I think you had a lot to do with that, Maddie." Mrs. Morrison was sure of it and felt proud of her daughter.

"I think I did have something to do with it, Mom, but it was mostly Teddy," Maddie said without thinking about how it might sound.

"Teddy who? Is it a boy on the team?" Mrs. Morrison asked.

"No, I mean Teddy Roosevelt," Maddie continued and tried to make sense of it for her mother. "You know, in our research we found out that Teddy Roosevelt had asthma as a boy, and when Bobby found out how he had become president and how he had worked to take control of his asthma, he figured he could do the same thing and well, yeah, that's what I meant. That report gave us more than just an A+ in social studies, didn't it?" Maddie's explanation was all anyone would need to see how Teddy helped Bobby. Of course she knew how much more there was to it.

"You certainly did get a lot more than just an A+, Maddie. I have seen a wonderful change in you. Your motivation for school and your excitement about history is fantastic. Like wanting to come with me today-- since when do you want to go to the antique store with your mom?"

Maddie explained her new-found interest in Teddy Roosevelt as the reason for wanting to go to the antique store and see the Roosevelt stuff there. She and her mom had a great conversation all the way to the store that included news about Audrey and Julie, Bobby's friendship with Maddie, and maybe taking some time tonight to work on perfecting the Sundae Surprise S'mores recipe. They pulled into the parking lot at the antique mall and Mrs. Morrison commented on how fast they had arrived.

"I don't remember it being so close to home. Maybe it was all our talking that made the time go so fast today, Maddie."

"I guess so, Mom. Let's get inside and see if they can fix the clock. I really feel bad about breaking it. Where is all the Roosevelt stuff? Do you remember?" Maddie asked hoping no one had bought the table yet.

"Sure, it's back over there, Maddie," Mrs. Morrison directed as they entered the store. The saleslady who had helped them last week followed them over to the table.

Maddie saw the table immediately. She was there in an instant to inspect the legs of the table. She remembered the legs most of all. She kneeled down and looked closely at the intricate work and knew this was the table.

She heard the saleslady greet her mom, "Hello, dear. It is so nice to see you again. How can I help you today?" Maddie looked up from below the table and could see the same skirt, and the back of the woman's head had the same tight grey bun. The only change was a crisp white high-collared shirt; otherwise the old woman looked exactly the same as last Saturday.

"Actually, the clock we bought has been damaged and I came in to see if you knew anyone that could do repairs on a piece like this." Before handing her the clock, Mrs. Morrison turned to look at the other pieces on the Roosevelt table. "Miss, did someone buy the vase that was here last week? It was such a lovely piece."

The saleslady answered without looking up from the clock, "What vase, dear?"

"The glass vase that was displayed here with this frame and the clock we bought." Mrs. Morrison was looking around the area to see if it had been placed somewhere else.

"I don't know anything about that vase. But we did get another Roosevelt piece in just yesterday, if you are interested. That chair just next to the table there." Maddie heard this conversation and jumped up from below the table hitting her head and almost knocking the table over. It brought back the same memory that had come to mind as her mother was inquiring about the vase."

"Be careful, Maddie. Are you all right? You

certainly don't need another blow to the head." Mrs. Morrison bent to see how she was, but Maddie quickly recovered and looked at the items on the table.

"There was definitely a vase here last week. I remember you asked how much all the items were, Mom. The vase was too expensive so you bought the clock," Maddie reminded them both as she began to put the pieces together. "But it's not here anymore. And the reason it couldn't be here is because it broke into a million pieces when it fell off the table." Maddie recalled the moment that Teddy banged into the table when he saw Bobby for the first time and the vase and the clock fell. Maddie remembered picking up the pieces of glass all over the floor when she saw the familiar clock and...

Mrs. Morrison interrupted Maddie's thoughts, "What do you mean it broke, Maddie. When did it break? Did you knock it over last week?"

"No, I didn't touch it, Mom." Maddie groped for a plausible answer. Maybe now was the perfect time to tell her mom about her time travel adventure. Mrs. Morrison would surely believe her story now that Maddie had solid proof. The missing vase! That was the ultimate proof. "This is perfect," Maddie added and her mom looked at her confused.

"Maddie, what are you talking about?" Mrs. Morrison saw the saleslady motion for her to follow her into the office. "Let me find out about fixing the clock and then you can tell me what is going on here. It's about time you told me what's been on your mind. I'll be right back." Mrs. Morrison had seen the difference in Maddie this week. It was all good. Maddie was happy and her grades were up, but something was strange and it was time to get to the bottom of it.

As they walked toward the office, the saleslady spotted a glass vase in a hutch display. "M'am," the saleslady called to Mrs. Morrison, "is this the vase you were talking about?" Both Maddie and Mrs. Morrison eagerly peered at the piece she had located. Maddie worried that if it really was the vase, then she wouldn't have proof of her time travel.

"Oh, yes, this is the one. Isn't it pretty, Maddie?" Mrs. Morrison remembered the intricate, floral etching in the vase and was thinking about buying it.

Maddie took a moment to think. She realized she had never actually seen the vase in Teddy's house before it smashed to the ground. Maybe the one that broke was a different vase after all. "Yeah, it is pretty. I guess it didn't break. I don't know what I was thinking, Mom." Maddie sighed, disappointed, and tried to cover up how crazy she must have sounded before.

"I'll be right back, honey. See if there is something else you like, but be careful not to break anything." Mrs. Morrison winked at Maddie and left with the saleslady.

Maddie knew she was there, with Teddy, in 1871. *If only I had proof, even just for myself.* Her thoughts exhausted her so she plopped down on the chair next to the Roosevelt table.

"Yeesh, this cushion feels like the horse I rode last summerrrr..." Maddie stopped short and breathed in deeply as she jumped up and almost knocked the table over. "Ahhh, I don't believe it! **This is the same**

chair!" She inspected it closely. She felt the scratchy cushion again as she called for her mother. "Mom," Maddie ran to the hallway. "Mom," she called again, louder.

"What is it, Maddie?" Mrs. Morrison hurried out of the sales office to see what had happened.

"Mom, I found something I like. Could we please buy the Roosevelt chair?" It was Teddy's chair and now it could be hers. It all made sense somehow. It was her proof!

"Maddie, it is the most uncomfortable chair I have ever sat on. The cushion feels like bristles," Mrs. Morrison said as she got up from the chair. She loved the look of the chair, but she wasn't sure if anyone would ever sit in it. The saleslady quickly followed Mrs. Morrison to take advantage of the possible sale. "It's horse hair, dear. It was commonly used on furniture of the time period. Having a piece like this in your home would be like traveling back in time."

Maddie laughed to herself, "C'mon, Mom, it would be like our very own time machine. A little uncomfortable maybe, but amazing!"

Mrs. Morrison looked at the price tag and raised her eyebrows, "Let's talk to Dad first and see if he feels the cost is worth a trip back in time."

CHAPTER 17

Time went very quickly that day after Mrs. Morrison and Maddie left the antique store. They picked up Audrey and Julie and got to Bobby's baseball game just in time to see him up at bat for the first time.

"Go, Bobby, you can do it!" Maddie screamed as she sat in the bleachers. Bobby looked up to see her smiling and cheering him on, just like she said she would. He felt stronger than ever and it showed as he hit a triple and started his team off on a hitting rally that lasted for three more innings. Mrs. Gordon had filled the girls in on how Bobby got in to the lineup so quickly. Their regular right fielder hurt his ankle in practice, and the team needed him to fill in.

"How is his breathing, Mrs. Gordon?" Maddie was hoping there were no problems.

"Perfect, Maddie. There have been no problems, but he has his inhaler if he needs it. I'm so happy he is playing." She smiled and put her arm around Maddie. "Mr. Gordon will be here any minute. He left work early to catch some of the game."

After Mr. Gordon arrived at the game, Bobby caught a fly ball and then there wasn't any more action out in right field. His team won and Bobby rushed over to Maddie after the game and whispered in her ear, "It sure took a lot of time to get to this point, but it was worth the trip . . . and you're the only one who knows what I mean. Thanks for being here, Maddie."

"I wouldn't have missed it. You were great. Oh hey, Bobby, I have to tell you about what happened at the antique store today. If we ever needed proof about our trip back in time, I have found it."

"I **know** we were there, we don't need any more proof." The way he felt at that moment was all the proof he needed.

"I know we were there, too. I wasn't even looking for any proof, Bobby. But I kind of just fell into it. I'll call you later and tell you all about it. Right now it's about you and your baseball." Maddie hugged Bobby and smiled. He tousled the hair on the top of her head and waved to her as he ran off to enjoy this moment with his parents.

Maddie, her mom, and the girls walked back to the car and sang songs all the way home. After they dropped Audrey and Julie at their houses, they talked about convincing Mr. Morrison to buy the Roosevelt chair. Neither of them was too sure how he would feel about it. He loved history, but he wasn't going to be too happy about having to pay so much money to own a piece of it.

"It's all in the timing," Mrs. Morrison confided. "I'll talk to your father later, Maddie. Let's get to your Sundae Surprise S'mores sample and recipe. We added a little something to your recipe, but I have to say you came up with a winner. You were the one who created it so you're the best person to tell me if it tastes just right."

"Okay, Mom, but I learned it all from you, you know."

Mrs. Morrison smiled to herself as she took out the samples left over from their meeting. She handed Maddie the sundae surprise one. It looked a lot better than the one she had made with Audrey and Julie.

"It looks so good, Mom. What did you add to it?" Maddie was looking closely at the scrumptious treat.

"Just try it and see if you can figure it out. It's not much different than your original recipe."

Maddie took a big bite. She chewed thoughtfully and paused. Her face lit up as she squealed and rushed to hug her mom. "It's icing, vanilla icing, for that extra creamy ice-cream-like flavor! You're a genius, Mom!"

"It's your recipe, Maddie. You worked hard and had plenty of fun doing it. Doesn't it feel good when all that work and fun pays off? You know what, Maddie?" Mrs. Morrison said as she reached in a drawer and pulled out a red marker. "This recipe deserves an A+." Mrs. Morrison put a big red A+ on the recipe card and posted it on the refrigerator right next to Maddie's history grade.

"Thanks, Mom. That's two A+s in one week for me. It's historic, don't you think?" Maddie grabbed the last of the Sundae Surprise S'mores and shoved it in her mouth. "And, now the s'mores are history, too!"

Sundae Surprise S'mores

If you don't have these items in your pantry, like Maddie did, then ask your mom to pick them up at the store:

Plain graham crackers
Jumbo marshmallows - 2
Plain chocolate bar – 2-4 squares
Caramel sauce - as much as you like
Jar of cherries – 1-2 cherries sliced
Vanilla icing – a lot or a little…it's totally up to you!
Colored sprinkles – You have to use a lot of these

Now get some of your friends and have some fun. Put it all together in a scrumptious treat just like Maddie, Audrey, and Julie did:

• Split one graham cracker sheet in two pieces
• Spread vanilla icing on the inside of both crackers
• Press colored sprinkles into the vanilla icing on each side
• Place one layer of chocolate squares on top of the sprinkles on one of the graham crackers
• Using a long fork or skewer to hold the marshmallows, toast up two marshmallows over the flame on a gas stove or a bar-b-q grill. (Ask your mom for assistance on this one. It could get very messy, but that's part of the fun!)

• Push the marshmallows onto the graham cracker.
• After licking your fingers, wash your hands and continue
• Drizzle the caramel sauce over the marshmallows
• I would definitely add more colored sprinkles over the caramel sauce for color-it's your choice
• Randomly place sliced cherries on top and then…
• Cover with the other iced graham cracker and squish down

• Watch as everything smooshes out and quickly take the first bite before someone else does

• ENJOY!!!!!